GW01606373

TAMRA

TAMRA

FAYSAL MIKDADI

MARTIN BRIAN & O'KEEFFE — London

First published in 1988
by Martin Brian & O'Keeffe Ltd
78 Coleraine Road London SE3

ISBN 0 85616 361 9

Printed in Great Britain by
Biddles Ltd., Guildford and Kings Lynn

By the same author
Châteaux en Palestine
A novel (La Pensée Universelle, Paris)
A Return
The Siege of Beirut
Poems (Martin Brian & O'Keeffe, London)

Tamra grew up in the [illegible] professor of mathematics at [illegible] Beirut. Her mother was a [illegible]

Mark [illegible]

almost [illegible] poetry. [illegible] have been [illegible] "I have met [illegible] when [illegible] be married [illegible] and [illegible]

Tamra was often sent to [illegible] but rather to the [illegible] of a [illegible] she became the [illegible] visitor [illegible] Pierre [illegible] when she told them [illegible] they needed to know about [illegible] truth beauty.

Tamra's father was at the [illegible] doctorate in his subject, before [illegible] marrying Marie. He was a keen [illegible] found it interesting to discuss [illegible] lengthy chats on equal terms [illegible] had married [illegible] the [illegible] At least that [illegible] Marie's influence over him [illegible] of getting round him. He always [illegible]

ONE

Tamra grew up in the lap of luxury. Her father was a professor of Mathematics at the American University of Beirut. Her mother was a graduate of English Literature.

Marie was a rapacious reader. Her reading consisted of almost anything she could get. But her main interest was poetry. Keats may have been talking of her when he said, "I have met with women whom I really think would like to be married to a poem, and to be given away by a novel."

Tamra was often sent to sleep, not by a nursery rhyme; but rather to the strains of a Keats poem. As she grew up, she became the family showpiece reciting sweet melodies at visitors' request, with her father looking on proudly. Even Pierre – a literary Philistine – failed to remain unmoved when she told them, with a glint in her blue eyes, that all they needed to know about beauty was truth, and about truth beauty.

Tamra's father was an educated man. He had obtained a doctorate in his subject before returning to Lebanon and marrying Marie. He was a keenly logical man. Marie always found it interesting to discuss things with him. They had lengthy chats on equal terms. Generally speaking; Marie had the Eastern woman's knack of allowing her husband the last word. At least that was what he felt. In reality, Marie's influence over him was substantial. She had a way of getting round him. He always thought that he had made major decisions. In fact, Marie had directed his thoughts her way.

Pierre was a mixture of a Western culture and an Arabness that at times clashed. He genuinely felt that there were certain things that were right simply because they had been going on for a long time. As a Maronite he passionately believed in his Lebanon. A vision of an independent and strong Lebanon whose relationships with neighbouring Arab states were to be on an equal footing. He had a strong suspicion and dislike of the Syrians whose ambitions over the Lebanon worried him. He thought that it was his duty to be constantly prepared in the face of Syrian provocation.

As a young man he had joined the Phalangist Party and enrolled himself in its military wing. He was fully trained for any contingency, although he managed to stay out of trouble during the first civil war.

Pierre's logical mind was able to discern things political in a way that many of his compatriots could not do. He felt that Lebanon's position in the Arab world was precarious. He fully understood Moslem fears of Western influence. His place of work was a hot house of political intrigue. Many of his most able and brilliant students were ardent Arab Nationalists. The Arab Nationalist movement had actually been started by Christian Maronites in the nineteenth century.

Pierre's was a world astride two cultures. On the one hand, his intellect told him that it was quite logical for the Lebanese Maronites to want an independent Lebanon free of Arab influence. It also told him that it was equally logical for the Moslems not to want such a thing, since their religion and culture were akin to their Arab neighbours'.

He somehow felt that it might not be far-fetched to think of a Lebanon on the lines of a Switzerland. Even then, he knew that it would take a long time before this could be achieved. His psyche was a throwback to the days of the Crusades. Emotionally, he was a Maronite through and through. Lebanon was the last enclave of Christianity in a hostile Moslem World. It needed to make an accommodation with anybody in order to survive. It did not matter who: the Americans, the Israelis, the Egyptians, even the detestable Syrians.

Such thoughts did not matter much in the Lebanon of the sixties. The country had emerged from the 1958 civil war with a new vigour and a will to survive. There were no victors and no vanquished. This formula suited the Lebanese business mind that went on to make its little fortunes. Beirut was expanding and becoming more and more colourful. Its life was busy in every way. The gap between the poor and the rich was widening fast but the municipality managed to cover the cracks cleverly and to maintain Beirut's cosmopolitan image.

Tamra was brought up in this bustling and prosperous atmosphere. By the time she was a little girl, Tamra went to an English-speaking school despite the strong social pressures on her parents to send her to the normal French-speaking one. Her mother felt that English was definitely becoming the international language. French may have been socially desirable. But without English Tamra was going to get nowhere.

And Marie wanted her to get very far. Marie was one of the first generation of liberated Lebanese women. She wanted her daughter to become independent, strong, and adaptable for the future prosperity of a new Christian Lebanon. She always tried to teach her how to take care of herself. Many of her bedtime stories were about Lebanese princesses whose passivity offended Marie.

One such story was of a princess who had refused to marry the prince chosen by her papa because she was in love with a pauper. Her father punished her by chopping off her hands. The princess sat beside the river weeping and moping. Without hands she could not eat. She soon expired. The father bitterly regretted what he had done.

He soon passed away.

'Mummy, why didn't the princess run away with the man she loved?'

'Because her daddy wouldn't let her go with a poor man,' answered Marie.

'It would've been all right. He was a prince really. He had a spell on him. Anyway, it wasn't nice to chop her hands off,' Tamra added indignantly.

'In the old days these things happened.'

She sat up in her bed with wide blue eyes and said, 'I don't think my daddy would do that.' Then she thought for a while and added. 'I wouldn't let him. I would defend myself. I'm strong. I beat Muhammad last week when he called me names.'

Marie felt a mixture of pride and guilt at her daughter's statement. Pride because Tamra was obviously going to be strong enough to look after herself. Guilt because Marie knew that for Tamra to talk that way about her father was wrong.

Tamra was growing up with an inner rebelliousness that her mother had to teach her to conceal. She told her stories about men and women who had to carry secrets within their souls for years and how these secrets helped to save lives and whole continents.

'It's important to carry secrets. "Any secret is your servant if you keep it; your master if you lose it"' she added proverbially.

Marie tried to bring Tamra up with a sense of her individuality. She also wanted her to learn the art of compromise.

Tamra's response was even more aggravated rebelliousness than the normal adolescent one. She grew up aware of her own perception of her rights as an individual. Nothing could detract from that perception; not even her mother's fear that Tamra would become an outcast in the male dominated Lebanese society.

But the relationship between the two was too strong not

to overcome this difficulty.

Marie promised Tamra her support in fulfilling her daughter's aspirations. In return Tamra made a solemn promise never to take any major action in her life without first consulting her mother.

This promise became part of their close friendship. In late adolescence it extended to Tamra's relationship with men whom she regarded as her equals. Such open equality, in Marie's eyes, meant socially unacceptable behaviour.

She extracted a new promise from Tamra. A promise never to allow this equality in sexual matters. Not till after her marriage.

Tamra, not seeing marriage as a possibility in her young view of the world, solemnly promised in order to please her mother and friend.

* * *

Jounieh. The hinterland of Maronite Lebanon. From above it: one of the most spectacular views in the world. For as far as the eye could see, a series of bays with sandy white and brilliant blue. Movement sandy white. Still brilliant blue.

And overlooking, shrouded in mist, haloed by myths; stood Our Lady of Lebanon; protectress, giver of mercy, and healer of all ills.

Paul was born in Jounieh. His infancy and childhood were spent growing up amidst strong Maronite aspirations and independence.

Before the days of electric lifts and tourist appeal; his mother would take him up to the top of the first range of the Lebanon mountains to visit Our Lady. The journey would take several hours of climbing the narrow path to the top. After saying a prayer and placing a short written appeal on the grill surrounding Our Lady; Paul and his mother would picnic awhile before visiting local friends.

Paul loved these excursions. They brought him nearer

to his mother. Much more exciting; they gave him the chance to join the Phalangist troops training in the hilly woods around the area.

The local Phalangist leader was a middle-aged man with wide shiny eyes.

'Have we got the biggest army in the world?' asked Paul one day.

'We're working on it my friend. And one day we will have an army that would be strong enough to kick out all the foreigners from Lebanon. Then, little brother, you will be able to walk safely anywhere in our country. Anywhere.'

'What are foreigners?'

'People who don't belong here. People who were never asked to come into our beautiful country and spoil its beauty.'

'That's not fair. Why can't they come here and take some of that empty land down there? That way we'll all live happily ever after.'

The leader laughed and patted Paul on the head. He motioned him to sit down beside him. Paul looked around and found a little rock that suited him and sat down overlooking Jounieh Bay and the distant shimmering colours.

'It's not as easy as all this,' started the leader. 'You see Paul, we have worked hard to make this beautiful country what it is. I don't mean that we laid the rocks or that we built the mountains. God does all that. But God made it so beautiful and so productive for us. And we were put here to look after it and keep it for Him. It's ours. So when someone comes in from outside and starts to do things that spoil it; then we don't want them here. They can go elsewhere.'

Paul's parents took him to the Cedars often to visit relations there. Apart from the breathtaking beauty of places like Besharri and the surrounding Cedars; there were endless walks and long stories told by his father.

His father, a keen hunter, would take him out very early in the morning. They would spend the day hunting; father with a shot-gun and Paul with a small pellet gun that was his pride and joy. They hunted birds mainly; although now and then they would come upon wild rabbits. As the sun rose, unfolding the rugged mountainous terrain; they would sit down to a simple breakfast of bread, olives, and onions.

In the winter; the landscape was bleak and snowy. Their only chance of getting game lay in waiting for hungry animals to come out searching for food. The trees were covered in purity with the flat Cedar branches shaking their snowy weight off. Terraced hills were immaculately clean in their thick, white, winter blanket.

But the main hunting activity took place in the summer. The sun scorched everything in sight. The rugged slopes around them gave off intense heat. Its soil always gleamed inordinately red. The only greenery around was the Cedars.

'Daddy? Why are the trees still green when everything else is brown?'

'Ah! That is an old secret my boy. A very important secret. You see, when God made this beautiful land he covered it with lovely trees. All these were Cedars. Whole mountains were covered in them. A long time ago, foreigners came and cut those trees down and took them away. God was not pleased to have his special – very special – land touched like this. To protect the trees He put a special spell on them: they would be evergreen and they would never burn. Ever.'

'Does that mean that if you put a match to the tree over there it would not catch light?'

'Right my son! That Cedar tree can't be burnt. No one can burn it except God. And the Cedar is made like us. We can never be burnt. We can never be taken out of this land. This is our land.'

Paul was impressed by the solemnity of his father's tone and by a click in his throat.

That night, while the parents and their hosts were

sitting outside drinking coffee and chatting; Paul and two of his cousins slipped out of their beds and out of the house.

'But Paul, they'll kill us. Dad would skin me alive for this.'

'Shshshsh! No one is going to know about it. It won't take a few minutes. And I told you I'll give you my sweets tomorrow if you help me.'

By then the three boys had arrived at the Cedar tree that Paul's father had pointed out that morning.

'Come on,' ordered Paul. 'Get a few branches and put them there near those stones. I've got the matches.'

The three boys crouched beside the green branches heaped in the middle of a few stones. Paul lit a match and placed it in their midst. Immediately a sizzling was heard and the flames went out. Paul tried again. The sizzling was again immediately followed by silent darkness.

He put the whole box of matches into the branches and lit a match placing it carefully on the edge of the box. A few seconds later there was a sharp crackling noise followed by a hiss and a strong flame. The flame lit up the three faces as they crouched with fear awaiting the result of their experiment.

'It's going out!' whispered a boy.

'They won't burn! They won't,' said Paul, with awe in his voice. 'It's impossible to burn them because God said so.'

'You know what's going to happen to you Paul. God's going to burn you for this. The Cedar is sacred. It's special.'

Paul did not say anything. He picked up the branches, walked back to the tree and tried to push them back into place.

A slight breeze shook the tree.

'Listen!'

'Did you hear that?'

'Yes!'

The three boys froze in silence. Suddenly Paul broke away and started to run home.

'Let's get out of here!!'

* * *

Winter. The mountains around Jounieh were covered in snow. The sea, still very blue at times, crashed against the bay bringing cold searing wind with it.

Paul's school were going on an outing to Beirut to visit the National Museum. The bus left very early in the morning for the short drive into the city. Passing the abattoir they held their noses because of the ferocious stench that came from the slaughter house along the highway. One of the teachers sitting at the front turned to his colleague and complained.

'You'd have thought they'd do something about that place. Does it really need to smell that bad?'

'It's not the abattoir, sir,' commented the driver over his shoulder. 'It's those bloody Palestinians living around it in Karantina!'

Both teachers laughed. Paul turned to his friend with a quizzical look.

'What are the Palestinians?' he asked.

'The dirtiest race on earth,' shouted the driver.

Paul looked at his teacher and asked, 'Who are they, sir?'

The teacher turned around in his seat, swung an arm over its back and looked at Paul with great distaste.

'They're a group of people who don't belong here, my boy.'

'Where do they belong then?' asked Paul.

'Somewhere in Hell!!' came the answer from the driver who was getting very annoyed by the boy's questions.

'Really sir, who are they?'

'Well, a few years ago some Jews came from Europe and established a homeland in Palestine. The Palestinians who used to live there ran away instead of fighting. They ran all over the place and many of them came here for a while waiting to return home.'

'Why don't they go back then?'

'Because the Israelis – they're the Jews who took Palestine – don't want them there. They got out and they can't go back.'

The second teacher turned around laughing. 'Anybody would think that they were invited here. We don't want them. And one day Paul, they'll have to go.'

'But sir, if they can't go back to Palestine, where can they go?'

'The Syrians and the Egyptians make a lot of song and dance about them. So they can have them. We certainly don't want them here. Never have.'

Paul looked out of the window at the outside wall of Karantina.

'Have you ever seen one?' whispered Paul to his neighbour.

'No. But my sister has. She says that they're very dirty and they smell. They have to shave their heads because of fleas and things. The men sometimes eat their children during their Moslem feast. They're going to kill many of us. My sister knows all about them.' The boy spoke with the pride and glee of someone who had inside and privileged information.

Paul was petrified at the thought of men eating their children. He had heard of animals that ate their young. The image of a father eating his son sent shivers through his whole body.

'Do they really?'

'Do they really what Paul?'

'Do they really eat their children?'

'Yes of course they do. They also have sauces made from their blood.'

'Did your sister ever see that?'

'Yes. Many times. She knows a lot of them.'

'I don't believe you. They can't.'

'You don't have to believe me. Ask anyone. It's known everywhere.'

'You're lying . . . Sir, Joseph says that Palestinians eat their children. That the men cook them and eat them for the feast. It's not true, is it?'

Both teachers burst out laughing and clapped their hands. The driver pushed his head backwards straining to get in on the joke.

'What did he say?'

'Paul wants to know if it's true that Palestinians eat their children.'

'Does he now?' asked the driver in mock seriousness. 'Well, I'll tell you. Why do you think they have the abattoir in there. Hey? I'll tell you. To cover up the stench made when the fathers cut their children's throats and drain out their blood. They usually boil them although some prefer them fried.'

He started to laugh aloud joined by the two teachers. Paul felt his insides turn over at the thought of someone like him being butchered and fried for supper. He felt a cold sweat run through him and a strong warm wetness go down his legs.

'Sir! Sir! Paul's done a wee-wee! Paul's done a wee-wee!'

The driver laughed even more loudly shouting. 'Ah! That would be the sauce!'

TWO

Barely seventeen, Tamra enrolled as a Freshman at the American University of Beirut.

Her Freshman year was remarkable mainly for her excellent results. The time came when Tamra had to make a decision on her major area of study. Her parents took her out for a meal in order to give her a relaxed chance to consider the matter carefully.

As they settled down for coffee; Pierre started the conversation.

'Now, you brilliant girl, any ideas what you're going to do next?'

'I'm not sure really,' answered Tamra; who was absolutely certain what she wanted to study. She was using her mother's tactic of leading Pierre's thoughts towards her own choice of Physics as her major. She had scored a grade 'A+' in her Science Foundation course.

Marie smiled at her daughter encouragingly. She knew where the conversation was leading.

'I was talking to Mr Shah yesterday,' started Pierre quietly. 'He said that, with your grades, you could do almost anything.'

'He's sweet. But I'm not so sure of that.'

'Come on Tamra. You've done brilliantly. The whole world's yours to choose from.' Pierre sat back as he might have done while talking to one of his students. 'You must have an inclination towards something. Let's start from basics. Sciences, Humanities, or the Arts?'

'Sciences definitely,' replied Tamra.

'Science. Good! Now we've eliminated several areas that we need not concern ourselves with . . . '

Marie smiled again and took her husband's hand.

'Which Science though?' asked Pierre tapping his wife's hand. 'Nursing? A B.Sc. in Nursing might come in handy. Or perhaps Zoology or Botany? What do you think?'

Marie looked at Tamra and winked in further encouragement. Tamra took her cue from her mother and answered. 'Well daddy I wasn't really thinking of these subjects. I am probably more mechanically minded in terms of my Science work.'

'Yes . . . Maybe . . . As I said before, my daughter could do anything . . . ' said Pierre slightly uneasily.

'I was thinking of Physics dad . . . ' said Tamra in a tentative and questioning tone of voice.

There was a long silence. Marie pressed her husband's hand. Tamra busied herself with twirling her napkin around her thumb. Pierre was obviously wrestling with himself. His Western self applauded Tamra's single-mindedness which, after all, was his own. His Lebanese self was throwing questions up by the dozen: who would marry a woman with a Physics degree? Who would be interested in a woman whose brain behaved like that of a man? All this may be perfectly all right in the U.S.A. but not in Beirut. Men liked to be men. And that was that.

Pierre cleared his throat and, again, tapped his wife's hand. There was something accusatory about the tap. Marie had not done her job as a mother.

'There are many serious problems here Tamra,' he started, adopting as fair a tone of voice as possible. He knew that Tamra was not going to be bulldozed out of her decision. She had to be coaxed out of it for her own good.

'There are some major problems . . . There isn't a single woman in the whole Department of Physics. You will find life very boring without friends of your own sex. It's a man's world love . . .'

Tamra could feel her anger rising. She tried to control herself as her mother's eyes told her to persevere in the discussion.

'But father, I don't quite see what friendships have to do with it. I'll still have my friends outside. My school friends. I will only be in there doing my work and not making friends. As for it being a man's world. Really father, it's about time that men learned that half the world are women . . .'

Pierre bent forward in his seat and rested his elbows on the table.

'Look Tamra; I don't quite see what this talk about half the world being women has to do with our discussion. You don't seem to realise that in choosing to study Physics you have chosen the area where you are going to be hampered by virtue of being the first woman to try it. Every person in the Department is going to resent your presence. This has been a man's domain for years.'

'But dad,' she answered. 'Why is it that those men should feel so threatened by my presence? As far as they are concerned a mere weak woman could not possibly be of any consequence in their all-powerful world.'

Pierre looked into her eyes as impatience tore within him.

'Tamra,' he said angrily. 'What chances do you think you are going to have in this society with a degree in Physics?'

'Presumably the same chances as I would have doing any other job. If I were good enough, then . . .'

Pierre interrupted. 'You know exactly what I'm talking about. What chances have you got of getting yourself a decent husband after you become a physicist?'

Marie, who had been looking from one to the other lowered her head. She could feel Tamra's anger slip out of control before she even spoke.

'Oh come on father. Do you really think that the be all and end all of my life is to get married to some fellow who hasn't got the guts to take me for what I am? There are things in life a damn sight more important than little men.'

Pierre's answer came quickly and quietly.

'Perhaps in your world my dear. But in your father's world women marry and build their lives around their husband's. And yours is your father's world as I'm sure your mother would have explained to you a hundred times.'

Marie did not respond. She looked up at Tamra with a face clouded over with misery. She had wanted her daughter to stand up for herself. But she had never anticipated such a frontal attack by Tamra on her father's values. Despite all this she remembered her promise to stand by her daughter whenever decisions were difficult. She turned to her husband and spoke quietly but firmly.

'Pierre, wouldn't it be a good idea to ask Tamra's tutor about this? After all, Mr Shah knows her work better than either of us.'

'Ah, I see. My womenfolk have gone against me. I know when I've lost. I surrender . . . For now that is. We resume the war tomorrow . . .'

Tamra laughed. 'Daddy, it's not a war. Just a little battle.'

'And the melancholy fit shall not fall . . .' recited Marie jokingly.

Pierre turned to his wife and smiled. 'I too know my Keats: "Woman! When I behold thee flippant, vain, inconstant, childish, proud, and full of fancies . . ." '

'Well, he obviously knew a lot about verse and nothing about women,' interrupted Tamra.

* * *

This was not Tamra's first major confrontation with her father. Although she always gave the impression of being at ease with him; she was very frightened of his insularity. She loved him dearly and feared hurting him. Yet she was adamant on going her own way in life.

During her Freshman year, Tamra had met and made very good friends with Leyla Salman. Both girls were doing a Science foundation course.

Leyla's family had moved to Beirut after the creation of Israel. As refugees, they had settled down in the Sabra camp. The children were hard workers. The two boys had joined the PLO: Rashid as a guerrilla and Imad as a trainee at a medical centre. Leyla went to the American University to study nursing.

The fact that Leyla was a Palestinian and a Moslem never entered into Tamra's feelings for her. The two girls spent hours discussing politics. Tamra had considerable sympathy for her friend's quest for her homeland, while Leyla understood the Lebanese Maronites' desire for an independent Lebanon free of Palestinian influence. Although the two views were opposed, in the girls' friendship they were easily reconcilable.

When Leyla's eldest brother, Rashid, had met Tamra, he had been correct and very polite. Tamra, not for the first time, had been pleased that a man had taken her for what she was. He seemed to admire her intelligence and to like her for her love of Leyla.

Just before the Christmas vacation, Tamra invited Leyla to her parents' luxury apartment in Eastern Beirut. Marie received her with great hospitality and courtesy. It did not matter much to her that the girl was a Palestinian and a Moslem. Marie herself was one of the old Phalangists who had argued for the restoration of a Palestinian homeland. She believed in Pierre Gemayel's ideal of a strong and independent Lebanon whose inherent Arab character could not be ignored. She also agreed with the party's founder that the Palestinians should be helped to regain their homeland. Apart from the humanitarian aspect of the case; this was the only way that the Palestinians were going to be shifted out of Lebanon.

As the three women sat having tea and chatting about the university and its people; Pierre came in. He said hello to his wife and Tamra and waited to be introduced to Leyla.

'Daddy this is Leyla. She is in my Science class.'

Pierre nodded and ignored Leyla's proffered hand.

'You are a Palestinian, aren't you?' he asked frostily.

'Yes sir,' replied Leyla.

'Where do you come from then?'

'Jerusalem sir.'

'That's not what I meant, my girl. You don't come from Jerusalem every morning to go to university.'

'No sir. I live in Sabra. The Sabra refugee camp,' Leyla answered defiantly.

'The camp,' said Pierre with distaste. 'So you must be on a scholarship, I presume?'

'Yes daddy,' hastened Tamra to end the embarrassing questions. 'Yes. Leyla has a scholarship.'

'From the government?'

'Yes,' lied Tamra.

'From our government,' added Leyla.

'Your government, my dear?'

'The Palestine Liberation Organisation, sir.'

Pierre got up and left the room. Marie shuffled her feet and excused herself. Whispers could be heard from the adjoining room.

'I must go now,' said Leyla.

'Look. I'll pop in tomorrow,' whispered Tamra.

* * *

The next morning, Tamra went to the women's hostel at the university. She found Leyla sitting at her desk working. She sat on her friend's bed.

'Leyla,' she started. 'I'm sorry about yesterday. I really am.'

'It doesn't matter really. I'm used to it.'

'I don't care whether you're used to it or not. It was horrible. It makes me feel ashamed of my family. I really am sorry.'

Tears welled in Tamra's eyes. Leyla sat beside her and put her arms around her friend.

'Come on love. There's nothing to cry about. I'm the one who should be crying. You've got to learn to ignore that sort of thing.'

'Ignore it? come on Leyla. That's what everybody keeps telling American negroes. That's what they kept telling German Jews. You can't ignore the way people treat you. You've got to stand up and fight for yourself. To ignore that sort of thing makes you bitter. Jews who ignored Hitler's anti-semitism and thought that it would go away paid dearly.'

Leyla had heard that argument before. But she believed in keeping her own counsel and getting on with the job. She hugged Tamra to her and they stayed in each other's arms. They were like two who had decided to become blood sisters and had, in the intermingling of their bodies, solemnised the sisterly contract.

* * *

On Christmas day, while Pierre and Marie had their siesta, Tamra took a taxi to Sabra to spend the afternoon with Leyla. The taxi driver dropped her at the outskirts of the camp. She walked the rest of the way.

This was Tamra's first time in the refugee camp. She was shocked by the very lack of the most basic amenities that she and her family so took for granted. Yet the camp was a short distance from her own luxurious apartment in Ashrafiyeh. On the other hand she was pleasantly impressed by the organisation of the place. It was like another country. There were schools, hospitals, little shelters, health centres, maternity care units and so on. Tamra saw women and children queuing up for water at corner taps. She felt out of place. The children waved and the women smiled. She was struck by the singular absence of men.

Leyla's family made Tamra feel welcome. Their home was a two roomed flat cluttered with their belongings. It was kept immaculately clean. Rashid was by then away in the south on a tour of duty. Tamra was frightened by sitting with the family of what her people called 'a terrorist'. The son was talked about as if he were away on holiday.

Tamra and Leyla went out for a walk after they had all drunk black, sweetened tea together.

'Your family are lovely Leyla. The did not even ask me where I came from or who I was. They just accepted me for what I am. It makes me feel even more ashamed of my father for what he did to you.'

'You shouldn't be. My family's behaviour is not entirely because they're nice; which I think they are anyhow.' Leyla was silent for a while before adding abruptly, 'This is niggertown Tamra. And niggers are flattered by the attentions of a white woman who would grace their hovel with her presence . . . I'm sorry Tamra. Don't get hurt. It all came out the wrong way. All I meant to say was that the disadvantaged don't have the knowhow of questioning people. They accept any alliance that makes them feel accepted no matter how temporary it is.'

'You're right Leyla. It was just the tone of your voice that frightened me. But our friendship is above all this.'

'I hope so.'

'You sound doubtful . . .'

'Not of you Tamra. I love you as I would a sister born and bred with me. And I know how you feel about me. Our love is strong. Our friendship is everlasting. But we're not above all this, love. We're not. One day this place is going to explode into some awful carnage. When it does, I, as a Palestinian, would be on this side of the divide; while you would be on the other side. It's not inconceivable that your gun would fire the bullet that would kill me or mine.'

'Never. Because I would never carry a gun. Oh God Leyla, the atmosphere is frightening!'

'This is the atmosphere that I have to live with every day of my life.'

They walked in silence for a little while. Tamra took a little box from her pocket and handed it to Leyla.

'I hope you won't be angry. It's a little Christmas present from me.'

'Christmas present? For me? Why should I mind? Christmas is a feast for us Moslems too . . .' She opened the box and took out a golden pendant. The pendant itself had a minute inscription. As she held it up she saw the word 'forever' swinging before her eyes.

Tamra took it from her and put it around her neck. Leyla adjusted it embarrassedly.

'Forever friends. There was only enough space to put "Forever". Will you always wear it for me?' asked Tamra.

'Yes. Forever. For us.'

The two girls walked on arm in arm. Their youth burning with the promise just planted within each other's heart.

Forever.

* * *

'Mum, what do you think I should do?' Tamra asked about her choice of university career.

'I promised you that when decisions were difficult I would stand by you. I have had endless arguments with your father over this. He is really adamantly against you doing Physics. I know how you feel, love. He is not simply being a chauvinist.'

'Yes he is mum. There really can be no reason why he should be so against it.'

'In your eyes perhaps. In his, he is only protecting you the way that he knows best. Whether we like it or not; our society makes certain demands of women. It is not yet ready to let us do our own thing. Marriage is our lot. Within that we can do whatever we want.'

'So why can't I do Physics?'

'Try to put yourself in the place of a typical Lebanese man. He dreams of marrying a woman just like his mother. She will bear his children. She will not compete with him or make him feel stupid.'

'And that's supposed to be nothing important,' flared Tamra. 'It means that I've got to be in his shadow all my life. I have something to offer too. I've done well. You yourself said that there is nothing that I can't do. Oh I know how it sounds. It sounds pompous and self-centered. Why shouldn't it be? I'm happy with what I am.'

'As you grow older you will learn that this is not the case. You will learn to compromise. To do your thing – your own thing – within the limits imposed by your society.'

'Compromise? What does that mean? Doing English Literature and becoming a lousy underpaid teacher in some crummy little school. Do you really think I want to spend the rest of my life parsing a sentence and reading Keats?'

Marie was silent. She too had wanted to study Social Sciences and make herself useful to her society. Her father had really stretched his liberalism too far in allowing a university career at all. The compromise was reading English Literature as most of her friends who went to university did.

For days afterwards Pierre maintained his sulky presence. He did not say anything more about the argument. He simply resorted to talking to everbody at home in monosyllables. He was critical of everything around him.

As always, his sulkiness was paying off. Silence was Pierre's best weapon. In a couple of weeks Marie was beginning to show the strains of this treatment. Tamra wanted a way out if only to help her mother. She saw her mother paying the price for her own stubbornness. She decided to see her tutor.

Mr Shah was a liberal-minded man who spent most of his time involved in political arguments. His passion was the period known as the Arab Awakening. He talked and wrote on the subject, not out of contractual obligation to the university, but rather because of a strongly felt passion for history. For the last two years he had been working on a definitive life of President Nasser of Egypt. The subject of his book entered every one of his lectures or tutorials.

Tamra knocked on his door and received the customary, 'Entrez mon enfant.' Mr Shah called people twice his age 'mon enfant'. He was a very popular man at the university. During times of crises he took his customary seat at the Uncle Sam's cafe and students gathered around to hear his endless analyses of what was going on. He had a fund of historical parallels to give them. He had distinguished himself by predicting the seemingly impossible. He was the one man in the whole university to refuse the theory that Kennedy was shot by a lone fanatic.

'Hello, mon enfant. Sit down. Sit down. I was expecting a visit from you, mon enfant.'

'Sorry to disturb you sir. I wanted to ask you about my option choice for next year.'

'As I said I was expecting a visit from you. Mainly because I'm a prophetic sort of fellow. Added to that was the fact that your father told me you would be coming to see me. Now, what to choose for next year? Ah! The answer is obvious mon enfant.'

'Is it sir?'

'Mais oui, mon enfant. You should read Political Science and that way you would be the first woman President of Lebanon. How does this prospect grab you?'

'It doesn't sir.'

'It doesn't? Failed again. My prophesies fly out of the window. Here we are poised on the verge of an awful war . . .'

'War?' asked Tamra, frightened.

'Mais oui mon enfant. A war. Une guerre. Al-harb. Der Krieg. Bellum. Bello. Bellavi. Bellatum. Bellare. Ah les Latins! They even made war sound good.'

'Do you really think there's going to be a war, sir?'

'Ah yes. My friend Nasser and I have been in constant touch on the subject. He has advised me to give up writing his biography. Start writing the history of Lebanon's coming war.' Tamra laughed as her tutor winked at her.

'Well mon enfant, so you want to read Physics?' he spoke seriously.

'Yes sir.'

'Good idea. Why Physics?'

'Because I like it and because I think that it would be useful for Lebanon.'

'To build bridges . . .' he said thoughtfully. 'We've got the bridges. It's the water under them that we can't quite forget . . . I'm annoying you mon enfant. All right. Listen. I'm on chapter six of Nasser's life and he is still a baby. At this rate Clarendon will have nothing on me. So I'd better get to the point and get back to Nasser. Must wean him by chapter seven . . . Of course you are right to assume that Physics would be useful to your country and to your people. You would probably become a second Madame Curie. And like Madame Curie you would probably die. Not of radioactivity because of a great discovery. But of sheer boredom. Because you will have nothing to do. Sad as it may be this is a man's world and you're not going to crash into it with a Physics degree. What you want to do is insinuate yourself into it. Compromise is the only way for women now. Otherwise the men will put up guards and fight valiantly for their misconceived and sick right to be top dogs. So let us try to find a way around this thing.'

Tamra was none too pleased. A way around it would lead to Literature and detestable collections of cackling and whining women.

'I see that you got another grade 'A+' in Mathematics.

Mind you, have you got anything other than an 'A+' in anything?' he added jocularly. 'Why don't you study Mathematics? You are only a step from Physics. By the time you graduate you could decide to do postgraduate work with specific relevance to Physics. Mon enfant, this is known as a back door into the very thing you want to do. Pierre, votre papa, would be ecstatic. After all, you're his girl and you have his brain. He couldn't quite get out of that one.'

Tamra smiled at him. 'You should have been a philosopher and not a political science teacher.'

'Non, mon enfant. Philosophy is honest. In politics I can lie as much as I want. The better a liar I am the more brilliant a politician I shall be when I become the first Moslem President of Lebanon.'

***

Pierre was very pleased with Tamra's decision to do mathematics.

'You would make an excellent teacher,' he said proudly. Marie winked at Tamra in an attempt to avoid another argument about her detestation of becoming a teacher or a nurse or anything to do with being a woman. Tamra was going to be Tamra and nothing else.

Tamra joined her Mathematics classes with a great zest for her work. As always, she did extremely well. There was considerable resentment from several of her male colleagues who could not hope to catch up with her. Although she did not consciously mind it, she was lonely at university. Were it not for her close and strong friendship with Leyla she might well have given up her university career. This friendship had to remain a secret from her father whose treatment of Leyla was never referred to again. Several of his Christian friends told him about his daughter's undesirable friendship, but he chose to leave it alone. As long as Leyla was not brought into his house; he did not object to

Tamra's adolescent relationships at university. Nonetheless, he kept a wary and distant eye on her.

One day, as Tamra walked into the lecture theatre, there were the usual lewd whisperings going on. She took her seat in the front and put her papers out in preparation for the lecture. A young man walked up and stood in front of her desk facing the rest of the class.

'Hello Tamra,' he said.

She looked up at him and saw him look over her shoulder at a group of men sitting at the back. He winked at them.

'What're you doing tonight? I've got tickets for the West Hall musical performance by the Greens.'

'What am I doing tonight?'

'Yes bright eyes.'

'Staying as far away from the likes of you as possible,' Tamra said loudly enough to be heard across the whole room. The men at the back burst out laughing and clapped their hands.

'Now listen my girl . . .' started the young man.

'No! You listen,' shouted Tamra. 'I don't know who the hell you think you are. But I suggest that you're in the wrong place. The morgue might be a better place for you.'

'Why the morgue?' shouted someone from the back.

'Because the idiot is probably brain dead!' answered Tamra flushing.

The young man was livid. He raised his hand as if to strike her.

'Go ahead. That's your only language. Brute force!'

At that moment another man held the assailant's arm and twisted it behind his back.

'Why don't you try it on me, brother?' he asked.

Everyone in the lecture theatre became very quiet. Tamra's assailant looked around defiantly and saw the man behind him.

'Come on Paul. We were only joking.'

'Find someone else who might better appreciate your

idiotic humour. Okay?'

The other man smiled feebly and walked off. The men at the back applauded and several shouted. 'One to you Paul. Fifteen love.'

Paul sat beside Tamra and asked, 'Are you all right, love?'

'First I'm not your love. Second I was perfectly capable of taking care of myself, thank you.'

'Phew! You really are something. So they were right?'

'Who was right?'

'Those idiots at the back. I heard them laying bets on their friend's chance of taking you out. Do you know you've just lost your chance of going out with Mr Universe himself? The Don Juan of our great campus.'

'Oh my God! Was I that near to the nightmare? I thought that he was produced by Schuller in his lab?'

'Probably was. That is why he is to utterly perfect.'

Tamra smiled at Paul. She liked his happy face. When he smiled there were little wrinkles around his eyes. His whole face changed and was spread over with a strong sense of kindness. He was about two or three years older than she was. He was fairly tall and slim although his shoulders seemed ridiculously wide. She assumed that he must be a sportsman of some kind. Her attacker was obviously frightened of him.

After the lecture they had coffee together at the Uncle Sam's. They spent a very long time talking about themselves and their backgrounds. Every now and then someone would come in and shout hello to Paul. He was obviously a very popular man.

'What're you studying?' she asked.

'I'm in my final year. Philosophy.'

She laughed. 'Sorry. I'm not being rude. It just seems strange that a Lebanese man would want to study Philosophy. I thought you were going to say Engineering or Agriculture. Why Philosophy?'

'That's the kind of question that drives me mad. When I

graduate I might be able to answer it. I suppose that there were so many questions I needed to answer. They weren't the sort of questions that Science could answer. I knew perfectly well why a ball went flying across a field when you kicked it.'

'Energy converted from potential to kinetic,' answered Tamra automatically.

'Is it? Thanks. I didn't know the right words for it. I took it to be a foot kicking and the ball responding. Anyhow, I wanted to answer the question further. Not what was the ball doing but rather what it *was*. What its very essence is. The ontology of the damn thing.'

'The what?'

'The ontology . . . And don't ask me what it means. Please.' They both laughed and looked into each others' eyes.

Tamra really liked him. He did not even show any surprise at her knowledge of Physics. He simply accepted it. And in the storm of isolation and loneliness, this was one port offering a haven of peace and acceptance.

Unconditional acceptance, she hoped.

THREE

Rashid set out of the camp very early in the morning. The sun had not yet risen. The Beirut sky was bright blue streaked with thin clouds and rising mist. The air was a cool gentle breeze coming in from the sea. Rashid headed towards the seaside road.

His way lay within alleyways between high buildings bent inwards into the road – so tiny and silent at that time in the morning. Rashid walked with a steady pace looking up at the few buildings that had the beginnings of life in them. A window opened here. Another closed abruptly. Several shutters were pinned against the outside walls; it being too hot even at night to want to shut them.

Now and then a man or a woman passed Rashid on their way into the city with their produce. Some balanced massive square trays on their heads piled with bread, cakes, croissants and other pastry that were destined to grace many a breakfast table of those still then asleep. Several trolleys made of wood were pushed towards the city centre. They were laden with country produce; fresh vegetables and fresh fruits so dear to the city's stomach.

There was as yet very little traffic. A few horse-drawn carriages rumbled down the road with their load of dairy produce. Now and then a cyclist passed by carrying newspapers and magazines.

As Rashid emerged from the built up areas onto the

seaside road; he saw a few boys running towards the sandy beach. He had a strong urge to run after them. He remembered the days when his father took him and Imad swimming. The water always warmed to his touch. Waves pushed into him and he pretended to be dead. There was a tremendous sensation of freedom and pleasant helplessness as his body rose and fell with the waves.

He stood for a little while watching the boys splash and listening to them squeal. As suddenly as he had stopped; he turned around and headed south. He had two days to get to his meeting place near the Israeli border.

Soon, the sun had risen and was blazing down on Rashid walking near the airport road. Around him, the sand was very red. It sparkled as it reflected the sun's rays. An aeroplane came thundering down towards the airport. He wondered how many Arab tourists it carried. How many men running away from their wives for a sex-happy few days in the mountain resorts.

He hated such people. He recognised in himself a touch of envy at their security and strong financial backgrounds. But he knew that his hatred also came from the way that the Arabs had abandoned him and his people.

He had seen and experienced Arab cruelty first hand. He had been in Jordan when King Hussein had unleashed his fury against the PLO. That was how most of his battalion had ended up in Beirut in the early seventies. For a while he was stationed in Syria and had seen the way Palestinians were confined to reservations. He had known the humiliation and bitterness of midnight police swoops in search of troublemakers.

Such treatment only hardened his resolve to regain his people's homeland. Until that happened, they would be destined to roam the earth from ghetto to ghetto. From pogrom to pogrom. Until their holocaust saved them and world-guilt gave them their homeland.

Rashid cut across eastwards towards the mountainous route. He started his ascent just as Beirut had sprung into action. From where he stood, he could see the city spread before him. The higher he climbed the more magnificent was the view.

At its highest point; the mountain overlooked all of the city shimmering in the haze of heat. Its coastline undulated into bays and juts. Beirut itself was a series of undulations. Tall graceful buildings towered over small exquisite red-tiled houses nestling all over the city. And Rashid, like everyone who had lived there, could not help being filled with a deep love for the happy, bustling, and very naughty place. Cosmopolitan to its very fingertips. Yet so paradoxically provincial.

He sat down for his meagre lunch amidst wild herbs and flowers. The air was full of the strong smell of thyme. As children, the Salmans used to pick the slightly fluffy green leaves and chop them up for salad. Hot and moist; they loved scooping it up with their bread.

The landscape around was rugged and rocky. At a distance, on almost every side, could be seen lush, green forests despite the recent lack of rains. Rashid knew these areas well since most of his training took place there.

He resumed his journey after a short siesta in the shade. As he reached the summit, fog started to rise and it turned fairly cold. He walked on southward knowing that he would be descending soon. The fog thickened forcing Rashid to stop until it lifted.

Once he had been sent out with two other guerrillas on a one week survival exercise in the middle of winter. They were two men and a woman with nothing but their clothes. They survived by eating anything that they could catch with their bare hands. Rashid had eaten rabbits, snakes, rats, field mice, and even cockroaches. During the night, the three would huddle together in their snow dug-out. By the third night both men were sandwiching the woman between them and deriving temporary heat and comfort by making love to her.

After one week they were picked up. The three went out

to celebrate after having washed and cleaned up. After a long evening of dance and drink, they returned to a small hotel by the seaside. Their attempts at sharing the woman were met with a series of hilarious embarrassments as all three could not quite manage things as they had done during their survival week. Survival sex had taken the fun out of things.

Rashid laughed out loud to think that his only successful sexual exploit was in the line of duty. His laughter echoed across the mountain slopes and returned to him merrily.

He felt happy. The sound of his footsteps pleased him: now gritty against stones, now soft, then harsh and soft again. At other times his feet made a regular pattern alternating two shuffles with one click.

The sing song of his footsteps accompanied that most quintessential of Lebanese voices of nature: the cricket chirping away tirelessly. It was not long before Rashid's brain fell into step with the two voices. First it started as a mental accompaniment to them. Slowly it took the form of words. Any words that came and that could be repeated along with his footsteps and the crickets. Soon the words needed meaning and inner significance as Rashid thought of yet another poem. A poem that he could think of without the constraints of social embarrassment. His PLO boss had always encouraged him to continue in his writing. He had explained that one line of poetry was worth two military victories. And most of his public poems were about Palestine, about the will of his people, and about their anguish in refugee camps.

A more closely guarded secret were his love poems and his poems about nature. His poetry was like the landscape around him: rugged, tortuous, and beautiful. Always painful yet shimmering with strong hope.

Brown red mountains with distant sparkling white peaks roll down into Beirut. Within the city move little grains of red sand each reflecting a new life. A new hope. Beirut burns. Feeds on her children cooked in her own hysteria.

As it shifts its colours. Laughs at the size of bees and commences the long fall into Hell. He falls and falls and falls.

Rashid woke with a start as dawn spread. He sat up. There, at a great distance, lay Beirut. Peaceful with no fall. He sighed and got up to wash his face at a nearby stream.

After breakfast; he started his descent towards Sidon. Very soon Beirut disappeared behind a mountain as he entered a small Druze village.

The village was built on a series of terraces going down the side of the mountain. Its houses were simple concrete dwellings of the kind found in many mountain villages.

Men were already out working the fields. Rashid entered the village and went to the first house asking for water. An old man sitting by the edge of a small terrace called out to him.

'Good morning son. Good morning.'

Rashid walked towards the man who indicated a chair beside him.

'Sit down and rest. Here. Drink some,' he added passing him a large flagon full of cool refreshing spring water. He drank plentifully. The water was sweet as its taste told of the many mountains and dales it had passed through.

'Heading south then, my boy?'

'Yes father,' answered Rashid.

'Not much work down there for strong young men.'

'Not looking for work father. Visiting relations in Sidon,' lied Rashid.

The old man looked at him with twinkling little lines appearing in the corners of his eyes. Rashid felt slightly uncomfortable for a few seconds. He felt that the old man could see through him; right into his innermost secrets and soul. As the man's smile widened, Rashid was filled with warmth for him. This man represented solid Druze loyalty, decency, and a strong sense of nationhood that transcended all time.

'Been walking long?'

'Since yesterday morning only.'

'Used to walk a lot in my younger days . . . For days. With mules loaded. Fruits. Vegetables . . . It was Turks then. Turks and their mercenaries. Turks then. Israelis now. Many of our people in Israel. And Syria . . .'

A long silence followed. The two men sat staring out at the terraces and listening to crickets chirp. The brown soil sent up strong vapours to the burning sun. In the distance the haze made every tree dance, looking as if dappled with water.

Rashid stood up and put his hand out to the old man.

'Must move now. Thank you father for your kindness.'

'You're welcome son. Maybe we'll see you on your way back from your visit.' The twinkle returned to the old man's eyes. He shook Rashid's hand.

Rashid's mind kept going back to the kindly old Druze with the penetrating eyes. He obviously knew where Rashid was going and why. Apart from anything else why should anyone walk from Beirut to the south? Why the detour into the mountains? The coast road would have been shorter and quicker. The old man knew. He knew all right.

Rashid by-passed Sidon and Tyre and headed south towards Beaufort Castle. He arrived at the plain below it as night fell. The Castle rose before him on top of its green and rocky hill. He sat down to rest before making his climb. He was much too early and doubted if his rendezvous would be there. No sooner had he sat down than he heard a noise discordant with night nature. His trained ear told him that the movement behind him was being caused by at least four, or possibly five, men.

He sat as still as possible listening intently. As soon as he perceived the noise to be at its loudest – yet still hardly discernible – he jumped sideways and rolled several times over and in under a jutting rock where he lay flat and waiting.

He lay under the rock all night. Now and then he would nod off into a sleep full of colours and noises from his long walk. He would usually start out of his sleep suddenly feeling the cold night air.

As night gave way to dawn, Rashid's eyes felt heavy and his limbs ached with the night cold. He dared not move since he had not heard the men leave.

Grass started to look greener and the rocks lost their night shape and became streaked and dappled with a million year history. Rashid edged his way forward cautiously. There was no one there. He wondered if the men had gone away during one of his naps. He was sure they could not have done so.

He stood up and stretched himself. He started his short trek towards Beaufort Castle.

'Don't move!' a voice sprang from behind him.

Rashid froze.

'Put both hands behind your head and turn around slowly.'

Rashid did as he was told. Four men and a woman faced him. He felt pleased that he had at least got that right. One of the men came forward and searched Rashid's pockets. He took out a crumpled bit of paper and took it to the woman.

She opened the paper, read it, and burst out laughing.

'Rashid Salman! You son of a bitch! You kept us up all night for nothing!'

Rashid's heart jumped for joy at the woman's distinct Palestinian accent.

'Come on!'

The men came forward and hugged Rashid. The leader walked off heading towards Beaufort. The others followed her.

After a quick breakfast in the Castle, Rashid was briefed on his mission by the woman. Nicknamed 'the Avenger', she spoke fast and in a terse way.

'Israeli patrols are coming into the Lebanese side. You are to find as many as possible and inflict as much damage as you can. That's all.'

Rashid was dying to ask whether there were others who had been sent out like him or whether he was alone. He wanted to know the point of the operation. Was it military? Or did it have a purely political motive?

But he was too well trained to ask anything. He knew that he would get no answers anyhow. He had been briefed on his mission and told exactly where his arms caches were.

After sleeping most of the day, he set out at night on his own. His pockets were empty except for his handful of cigarettes, U.S. army issue lighter, and an empty holdall. The rugged terrains around him were to be his foodstore and his bed. At night the stars took on a friendly aspect and in the day a few frightened animals were his companions and friends, little suspicious that they were to provide his staple diet.

He went straight to the first cache given him. Removing the weaponry and putting it in the holdall over his shoulder, he started a steep climb over a small rocky hill overlooking the southbound road. Above him hung a small round rock that protruded precariously outwards.

Waiting all night and all through the next day, Rashid had ample opportunity to dream and think. He knew that he might die on this mission. He had mixed feelings about this. On the one hand, he did not mind dying since both his training and his circumstances taught him to accept death as inevitable for Palestinians. Whether it was going to be him or someone else did not really matter.

But on the other hand, he feared death because he feared the unknown. He was no more religious than any other of his compatriots. His obedience of Islamic laws was more cultural and traditional than religious. Death was the big unknown. He thought of the French revolutionary dictum that death was eternal sleep. And it was that eternity that terrified him. An eternity of blackness, thoughtlessness, and cosmic silence.

Late in the afternoon of the second day two armoured cars came racing down the road. Each carried six heavily armed soldiers. Rashid calculated the exact spot for a perfect hit: a large pothole by the roadside.

The moon was very small and without light. Rashid had to travel down to the road slowly and carefully. His long training gave him the qualities of an alert nocturnal animal. He thought, with a slight revulsion, of the raw rabbit he had lived on for a night and a day.

Approaching the road carefully, he found his large pothole and placed the explosives within. He gently placed soil and small stones around the mechanism and over it. Using a short tree branch, he quietly swept the soil and the road moving backwards into the route he had previously come from.

He returned to his vantage point and lay flat on his stomach. His mouth felt dry but he did not want to move. He drank the small droplets of water coming from the small rock above him.

He waited for hours looking up at the sky and wondering at the vast expanse enveloping him. He thought of Leyla and her friend Tamra. Her large wide eyes had always impressed him although he had only spoken to her a few times at university. To wile away the time, Rashid tried to compose a sonnet to her. Before long its soppiness embarrassed him but he persevered, comfortable in the knowledge that no one would read it. It was too full of 'my thoughts turn to you my sweet' and 'our hearts each end of life's love's beating.'

Somehow, alone, under the midnight sky, it did not matter. Soppy poetry warmed him just as those Palestinian martial songs moved him amidst crowds.

Silent crowds all staring. Lined up geometrically. Heads shaven. Bobbing. They lack colour: grey, with grit in their eyes and on their faces. Some have snakes twirled around their necks without loss of breath. At a distance rises a cloud of smoke getting bigger and bigger. Still all is silence. Silence. Out of the dusty clouds flounders an old rickety car. Its noise is deafening.

Rashid woke with a start. He rolled over onto his stomach just in time to see a convoy of armoured cars passing the pothole. He snatched his remote control and pressed the button.

He saw the cloud of smoke rise amidst the flash just before he heard the explosion. One car overturned. All the cars at the front speeded up and moved off. Those behind stopped, some turned left and some right and moved off the road their guns firing in all directions.

The cars that had speeded off did the same a few hundred metres down the road. One of them turned around and raced back towards the overturned car. Several men jumped out and ran towards it.

Amidst the noise of cars and machine-gun fire, Rashid could hear men screaming. Three men were laid on the side of the road.Two crawled out and stood up unsteadily.

All the cars stopped at the bottom of the hill. To his right Rashid could hear a swishing sound. He looked up and could just see two helicopter gunships swooping down towards the area.

One helicopter landed near the road. The injured men were speedily put on board and it flew off. The second helicopter swooped down from the hilltop firing incessantly. The armoured cars below also opened fire on both sides of the road. They continued to do so as they moved uphill.

Rashed slid in further beneath his rock and lay as low as possible. After several minutes of shooting, the helicopter headed out west to the sea and the armoured cars moved north taking their original route.

A deep silence descended all over the hillsides. The whole incident did not take more than ten minutes as day broke. Yet Rashid felt exhausted as a release of tension took place.

After about an hour, Rashid emerged from his hiding place and headed west over the hill towards his next cache. He climbed to the very top of the hill and started to descend westwards in search of his food.

Using his holdall and a few picked greens he sat back waiting patiently at the entrance of a small rabbit warren.

Some two hours later a small grey rabbit emerged tentatively and sniffed at the bag. It seemed to stand there for a very long time before putting its head inside.

Quick as a flash Rashid closed the bag and picked it up. He put his hand in. It emerged holding the rabbit by the scruff of the neck. One quick blow, a sharp squeal, and it was dead.

After his uncooked meal, Rashid started his walk again. He had not moved a few minutes when he heard the familiar swishing sound of several approaching helicopters. He dived for cover and waited. Before long he could hear the voices of men and the barking of dogs. Having landed their men and dogs, the helicopters started hovering in an air search.

Rashid knew that he was lost. The open terrain offered very few hiding places from men and virtually none from dogs. He was unarmed. He had only carried out one mission. But he was too well trained to consider this anything more or less than the fortunes of war.

'Come out!!' shouted a voice accompanied by the fierce barking of a dog. Rashid could see the man's legs.

He crawled out and stood up facing several men.

'Lie on the ground!'

He was frisked, undressed down to his underwear, blindfolded and bundled onto a helicopter with his hands tied firmly behind his back.

It was with sudden horror that Rashid realised the humiliation and indignity of his situation. He had hit alien soldiers on another country's soil. He was being taken out of that sovereign country into another. And that 'another' was his own homeland.

He looked like one of those sad yet comic little Palestinian prisoners parading in their pants on Western television screens.

FOUR

In Beirut, April had always been a very special month. The university campus bloomed in its full glory. Tamra and Paul took long walks through the campus. Their time was full of spacious days punctuated by the high dramas of events relating to student life. They often went swimming on the university's beach in a secluded area they called their own. Climbing a few rocks, they were able to swim a short way out into a distant and personal world, full of jutting rocks and small enclaves.

During the beginning of April, things had become a little strained between the two friends because of Leyla.

'Do you have to see so much of her?' asked Paul sitting in their little area.

'Why shouldn't I?'

'Come on Tamra. She is not one of us.'

'What do people mean when they talk about us? Who are we? Some chosen people? For goodness' sake, Paul, she is just like me and I'm one of us. Ergo she's one of us.'

'You know exactly what I mean Tamra. As a Palestinian her interests do not lie in keeping Lebanon safe and stable. Her people's actions will land us in an awful war with Israel. Have you seen how they behave in the south? Only last week they executed a girl for espionage!! Have you ever been there?'

'As a matter of fact, no I haven't been to the south.

Their behaviour has nothing to do with Leyla.'

'Of course it has. If my people behaved in a certain way, whether I'm with them or not is irrelevant. Their behaviour is equally my responsibility.'

Tamra patted him on the head and, smiling, said, 'Yes of course. You're a social animal par excellence, aren't you? But, mon enfant, I happen to disagree with you. My soul is my own and not my people's whatever that means.'

She jumped up and ran into the water. Paul followed her in and tried to push her under. She fought him. Eventually, he succeeded in carrying her out of the water. As they emerged from the sea he suddenly felt the weight of her body and started to sink into the watery sand. Tamra held on to his neck and both fell in. They emerged laughing and splashing each other.

They lay on the sand holding each others' hands. Paul leant over and looked at Tamra.

'You have beautiful eyes. The colour of the sea.' He came closer as Tamra stroked his face.

'I love you.'

He kissed her gently. His wet hair dripped on her forehead as his kiss became more intense. She held him to her.

'Paul. Paul. I love you too.'

His hand went over her neck and down to her breasts. He pushed her swimming suit down and kissed her again. His mouth touched her breast as she felt him with gentle strokes. His reactions did not frighten her as she had always thought they would.

She wanted him. She wanted him very much. Although she did not respond much to his advances, she felt herself carried by a wave of breathless love she could no longer control.

He pulled her swimming suit down her legs and kissed her again. His hand roamed over her whole body still glistening with water. He gently pushed her legs apart as his intensity began to overwhelm her.

'Tamra. I want you. I've always loved you.'

There was something trite about his declaration. Yet she loved it. She wanted to be his.

'Paul,' she whispered as her heart beat fast. Her whole being was suffused with a new feeling of warmth; his body pressing against her nakedness.

Her mind flashed a series of images. Her childhood. Her thoughts on love. Her mother.

'No Paul. Stop Love. Please,' she whispered urgently.

Paul leant beside her naked body stroking her face. He smiled.

'I'm sorry,' she said. She stood up and started to dress herself.

'Are you angry?' she asked timidly.

'I love you,' he pleaded trying to hide his impatience as he walked into the water followed by Tamra.

They went to the Uncle Sam's. They could not hold hands or show their love in public. Yet they both radiated an inner happiness that any discerning eye could see.

As they sat down side by side, Leyla came in and joined them. Paul was very nice to her. He hated no one. He felt nothing but his love for Tamra. They chatted about the university and various news of the approaching examinations.

'Mr Shah has almost finished his book on Nasser,' said Layla.

'When is it coming out?' asked Tamra.

'By Christmas I think. He was ever so excited this morning when he told us. Do you know he's been working on it for over four years. He had tears in his eyes when he told us about writing the death scene.'

Paul laughed. 'You make it sound like a play. It's a history book.'

'You're right. But in Shah's hands it is a narrative history. The best kind. About people. If he could jerk a tear out of his reader, he would. He has a strong feeling for the dramatic.'

Tamra told them about that time, so long ago, when he said to her that war was on its way. 'The prophet failed in this one, thank God. We aren't in the mood for a war now thank you.'

'No we aren't,' smiled Paul and looked at Tamra lovingly. Leyla caught their look. She flushed a little and smiled at Tamra. Tamra took her hand in hers.

'Oh Leyla . . . I'm so happy.'

Paul burst out laughing. Tamra and Leyla joined him.

A car screeched to a halt outside the cafe. Two men and a woman jumped out and ran towards the entrance. A traffic officer shouted after them, 'Hey you. Move your bloody vehicle off these lines. Now!!'

One of the men looked around and put a finger up at the officer.

'Go fuck your mother,' he screeched.

They ran into the Uncle Sam's. Seeing Paul they raced to his table breathless.

The policeman stood beside the car looking a little worried. A few seconds later he made up his mind to fight this one out. He followed the group into the cafe.

'Hey you three. I'll give you one minute. If that car isn't moved I'm having it impounded!' His pride was welling up within him as the customers sat back in comfort to watch the performance.

Paul looked up at his friends, 'Move the car, will you?'

The driver breathlessly said, 'Tell him to go fuck his mother. I'm not moving it. We've got more important things to do. Come on Paul, let's go.'

'Go where? Take it easy everybody. Come on, what's going on?'

The policeman had reached the table by then. He looked frightened enough to be menacing.

'Come on Paul. The whole world has gone up. There is a hell of a fight at Ain-el-Rummaneh . . .' said the woman.

'Ain-el-Rummaneh? What's happened there?'

'Where have you people been? A group of fucking Palestinians killed one of ours. Pierre Gemayel's people let them have it. At least twenty of the shits have been killed.

Come on Paul. This is war!'

Leyla's face turned pale. She looked down as the tears welled up. Tamra held her hand and pressed it. Paul got up saying to the officer, 'All right brother we're moving the car.' He walked off with his friends.

Tamra called after him. They met in the middle of the cafe as people started to talk animatedly analysing what had happened.

'Where're you going?' she asked.

'Back to Ashrafiyah. We've got to get ready.'

'Ready for what Paul? Please don't go.'

'Look Tamra, before long there will be hordes of mad Palestinians descending on us like a bunch of Apaches. We've got to get ready for them.'

'Paul please. It's not our fight. Please stay.' She would have done anything to keep him with her. Her whole body ached with regrets at not having gone as far as they could have on the beach. That might have made him hers. Fully hers.

'Tamra, these people are my people. They need me. They are your people. You're one of them. You must come too. You can't just pretend it has nothing to do with you.'

'I'm not responsible for what my people did. For God's sake Paul, we started it . . .'

'I'm glad you've said "we". Because it is "we" whether you like it or not. Are you coming?'

Tamra looked at his face and wanted to say 'yes'. She wanted to be with him whatever happened. It did not matter what the background was. She turned around and saw Leyla sitting at their table with her head still down.

'Come on Tamra. We've got to go . . .' Paul saw her looking at Leyla. 'Look love, she'll have to go to her people. Just as you and I have to do. Let's go.'

'No,' whispered Tamra. 'I'm not going. I'm staying with Leyla. I'll see you later. I'll come later. Please Paul, I need to be with her. If this goes the way you people are making it go; I want a last moment of peace with her . . . I want . . .'

Tamra's eyes filled with tears.

Paul put his hand on her cheek and smiled. 'You're right, of course. But it isn't in our hands anymore. If we don't get ready they certainly will . . . You stay. It'll be safe enough for a while. Stay love . . .'

He jumped into the car with his friends. Tamra saw him through the window mouthing 'I love you'. She felt momentarily happy. Yet her heart was heavy. Very heavy with what she knew was yet to come.

* * *

'What are you going to do now, Leyla?' asked Tamra as they sat in Leyla's little university room.

'I've got to go back to the camp. Must make sure mum and dad are all right. I'll carry on with my studies and help as much as I can in my spare time . . . What about you?'

They looked at each other. Leyla's heart was fit to burst as she threw herself into Tamra's arms. The two held each other tight. Leyla felt her friend sob against her.

'We'll be all right Tamra. You know we will.' Leyla pushed her away and held her face.

'Look at me,' she said. 'Look at this pendant. Do you remember when you gave it to me two Christmases ago? I've worn it ever since. And I shall continue to wear it until my dying day. One day, when all this is over – and it will be over – we will laugh at it. I'll still be wearing the pendant. You and I will sit on a balcony chatting with our grandchildren driving us mad with their noise. We will laugh at ourselves for crying now.'

'Oh Leyla. I wish we were the same . . .'

'Yes. We could be together then without worry. But we are the same. Only our stupid labels are different . . .'

'I love you,' whispered Tamra as she felt time running short.

'I love you too. More than you can ever imagine.'

The two women held each other for a long time.

* * *

Shah closed his folder on Nasser's life and stretched out his arms. It had been a good day's work. Over ten thousand words. He reflected that, at this rate, he should finish revising and tidying up the book in no time. He looked at the stack of papers bulging out of the file and his heart was filled with pride and satisfaction.

Outside he could hear the rumble of distant guns firing somewhere in the mountains as they had done most of the afternoon and evening. As always he could see many parallels to this war. The Maronites were getting the upper hand in a way that no one had anticipated. Shah knew that this was only a temporary thing since the Palestinians and the Lebanese Army had so far tried to avoid getting heavily involved. As soon as they stepped in, the Maronites would be crushed. And what next? The only parallel that he could think of readily was Poland all through most of its history. As Lebanon disintegrated, its neighbours would start carving her up. Eventually Israel would have the south and Syria the Bekaa and the north. Small Christian and Moslem enclaves would become scattered across the mountains and up and down the coastline.

Shah sighed and lit a cigarette. He wondered, for the umpteenth time that week, whether he should take his wife and son away. Many people were beginning to leave. Perhaps he could go to the States and do some research until all this is over. He would have to talk to his wife about it in the morning.

He felt tired but satisfied. He so wanted his wife to be awake so that he could talk to her about the book and then maybe make love and chat some more. He got up and left his study. He showered and went into his son's room. The little boy was fast asleep on his back with one arm flung over his eyes. He looked so innocent and trusting in sleep that Shah made up his mind there and then to leave Beirut as soon as possible. This was no place to bring up the lad and if he knew his history, this war was going to go on for years to come. The boy would be a young man before all this was over.

He went into the bedroom where his wife lay asleep. He sat on the edge of the bed and kissed her on her forehead. She moved and smiled. He kissed her again. Her lips responded gently as he pulled the covers back. She started breathing heavily as she clutched his body to hers.

She felt warm and inviting. He felt firm and cuddly. They made love slowly, now and then opening their eyes to look at each other. As she felt their orgasm approach she moaned and hugged him to her. It was one of those times when she just enjoyed him coming. Her own orgasm was second to his. More controlled. He always felt a little guilty at her seeming lack of response and had to remind himself of the time when she had explained to him that a woman's sexual response varies from day to day. From minute to minute, he had jokingly replied. Her erogenous zones seemed to change every four and a half seconds.

He turned over onto his back and they lay side by side.

'That was lovely you gorgeous cuddly bear!'

'Thank you. You're not so bad yourself mon enfant.'

'How's Nasser?'

'Fine. He's not far off dying again.'

'But he died last month!'

'This is a revision death my dear. A death almost as satisfying to my authorial vanity as what you and I . . .'

'Stop it you naughty man or I'll smack your authorial vanity most heartily.'

He turned over on his side and kissed her cheek. She stroked his face and whispered, 'I do love you.'

'Me too,' he laughed.

'Daddy! Daddy!' came a terrifying screech from his son's bedroom. Shah jumped out of his bed and ran.

His son was slumped across his bed with a huge red

gouge in his neck. Beside him stood a man with a knife and on the other side stood two men with machine-guns. Shah took all this in within seconds. Before he could even move or respond, the three men ran forward and one of them hit him across the head.

'Nasserite bastard!!'

As he fell forwards he felt them pick him up. He heard the crash of glass as he felt himself fly out of his son's window. The fall seemed endless. When it came, the thud was noiseless and painless.

As Shah lay on the pavement twitching regularly, he could hear his wife screaming.

* * *

Tamra did not see much of Paul for a very long time. He was stationed in Jounieh, where he led a small band of militiamen in defence of their Maronite homeland. She worked with the Red Cross as an ambulance driver. Before long she was used to the all-night vigils as she awaited calls to go out and pick up injured men and women. She could never get herself used to their sufferings. She found it hardest to handle children. They almost always sat in the back of her ambulance with a resigned look on their faces. They accepted their fate as part of the growing up process. Their little world maintained its feeble fiction of self-defence. Tamra would have found it easier to deal with crying or screaming children. But these were so impassive.

Whenever there was a lull in the fighting she was able to continue her studies. During the day, she would go into the university and return home in the evening to don her ambulance driver's uniform. Somehow, her university career had ceased to matter much to her. She continued it fairly successfully purely on her wits where others were failing miserably because they could not maintain the two lives.

Now and then she would meet Paul. His character was hardening almost daily. They would meet in Jounieh where he had a small flat.

'Tamra, let's get married.'

'I couldn't. Not yet.'

'Why. not darling?' he asked. 'Nothing has changed for us. It is the same as that lovely day on the beach. I want you for my wife.'

'I'm not ready yet. What's happening around us frightens me. Do you want to bring children into a world like this? Oh Paul why don't we go away? We can go somewhere away from all this and start a new life.'

'I'm not going anywhere. This is where I belong.'

'I understand. Honestly I do. It's just that I really don't feel that this is my fight. It has nothing to do with me. I never asked for it. I never wanted it. I don't want it. We were all right before this whole business started.'

'And we'll be better off when it is finished. Tamra, we are not fighting a futile war. We're not having fun. Sure, there are many who are like a bunch of cowboys having a great time. We are not. We are fighting for Lebanon. We are fighting for a better homeland. Our homeland, free of foreigners. Free of trouble . . .'

Tamra could not accept this. Every time she thought of a Lebanon free of foreigners, she thought of Leyla. Leyla was that foreigner. Yet Leyla was her sister. She was not going to be part of getting rid of her and her people.

Paul kissed her and she responded as always. He held her hand and took her towards his bedroom.

'No Paul. No.'

His anger rose. He kissed her again trying to get to her through his kisses where he knew words would not work. And his kisses almost did.

'I'm sorry Paul. Not yet. It's not right yet. Please don't be angry.

But he was getting angry. He could not understand what her objections were. He loved her and she loved him. That seemed such a simple equation to him. At one point he had almost tried to force her into bed after a particularly long absence during which he was on constant active service. He was the desperate soldier pleading for bliss in case he died the next day. Tamra still refused although they spent a whole night in each other's arms. She would not undress. This was the last time that Paul tried to make love to her.

'Tamra, what is it you want? Don't you love me?' he asked in despair.

'Yes I do. Oh darling, I do love you so much. I shall never forget our first kiss on the beach. I wish I had said yes then. It would have been during a clean and happy time. The world is so dirty. It is so sordid; I can't. I'm made impotent by what I see. Oh Paul, do let's go away .. You make me feel as if I had nothing to do with your passions. As if I didn't belong to myself. I want to give and not to be taken . . .'

A keen philosopher's mind saw the meaning of her words. A man desperately in love saw nothing but his desire for his loved one.

And they parted again. Sorrowful, repentant, and frightened of their next meeting not taking place.

Tamra's father gave up his job at the university and donned his uniform. He left home at any hour of the day or night whenever he was needed. Marie never asked where he was going or what time he would be back. She accepted the war and its consequences without fuss.

'I want you to go away for a little while,' Pierre announced one night to his family.

'Go where father? Why?'

'Please don't ask me any questions. I must have you somewhere safe for a while. Things are going to happen . . .'

An attack on Ashrafiyeh was unimaginable. Yet Pierre was implying just that. Tamra refused to go, 'I'm needed here dad. We haven't got enough people for ambulances. I must stay. I'll be careful. Don't worry.'

Next morning, Marie went to the safety of Damour on the outskirts of Beirut. She stayed with distant relations of hers and soon discovered why she had to leave Ashrafiyeh.

The whole neighbourhood came under very heavy bombardment.

Late one night, Tamra was woken up by a summons to drive her ambulance to the abattoir area. With tired eyes she drove in a convoy of cars and trucks. The convoy was hailed at a short distance from the shantytown of Karantina and its personnel asked to wait for further orders.

Inside the shantytown, people of mixed races and religions were asleep, their only thing in common was their appalling poverty. Morning dawned with thick, low clouds turning everything gritty grey. Just outside the shantytown, lines of Christian soldiers prepared for their surprise attack. Little resistance was anticipated. Most of the Palestinian fighting forces were diverted to the camps. Tal Zaater camp was preparing to defend itself because of rumoured attacks.

Pierre led his men and women into the wet rain-sodden shantytown. Soon doors were broken down and inhabitants dragged out of their beds screaming and pleading. They massed them in various small squares. Armenian Christians were allowed to walk out of the shantytown unmolested. Some Lebanese were also allowed to go.

All Palestinian men and many Moslem Lebanese men were herded into small groups and shot. Some tried to haggle and plead for mercy only to be kicked and punched against walls and shot.

'Let them go!!' shouted Pierre to a group of young men and women who had lined up six Palestinians against a wall.

'The motherfuckers are Palestinians, sir. We have orders to kill the bastards,' shouted a woman. 'We're going to make them eat their fucking children cooked in oil!'

'You heard what I said. Let them go! You,' he called to an elderly Palestinian. 'You! Lead that lot to the main road outside. There are trucks to take you to West Beirut. Come on! Move it!'

The old man started to hobble away from the group. As he passed Pierre he took his hand and tried to kiss it. 'God protect you and yours my son. God protect you.' He trembled as he spoke. He turned to the others and shouted, 'Come on! Let's go!'

Pierre walked away to make sure that the operation was a clean one everywhere. They were there simply to drive the inhabitants out. Not to massacre them. As he turned the corner he heard a simultaneous burst of gunfire and screams. He turned around and ran back. He saw the woman who had answered him back straddling the twitching body of the old man. She held his penis pulled up as she clumsily tried to cut it with a small penknife. Pierre ran up to her and kicked her on to the floor.

'I ought to kill you, you bitch. You had orders to let them go . . .'

'I'll never let a Palestinian prick go. Never!' she screamed back at him. 'I'll cut their fucking balls off and make'em eat them!!'

'You will obey orders,' shouted Pierre. 'Or you will find yourself hanging from the end of a rope. Do you understand that?'

The woman got up and nodded. She walked off with her group and speedily got out of Pierre's angry way. He stood looking at the six men lying before him. Who were they? What were their families doing? What were their names?

Tamra's convoy had been sprung into action. The trucks came forward and militiamen herded their prisoners into their backs. Palestinian and Lebanese women and children were squeezed into the back and driven to the Green Line dividing the city into its Western and Eastern sectors. They made their way across on foot.

Tamra made several journeys with injured people. She dropped them on the Green Line where others carried them across and threw them in the middle for West Beirutis to pick up.

On her third journey out she was stopped by a group of Christians. She recognised them as the Guardians of the Cedars, a small splinter group.

'Hello sister. Who have you got in the back?' asked one of them.

'Some people from Karantina. They've been injured. I'm taking them to the Green Line. I've got orders to do it,' she added knowing the futility of explaining.

'Let's take a look sister,' said another. He walked around the back and opened the doors. In the ambulance lay three people. Two men and a woman.

'Get out!!' he screeched.

'They can't,' protested Tamra. 'They can't walk.'

'They can be dragged then, can't they?' he shouted back at her as he dragged the first and nearest out. The man was almost unconscious. He moaned as his body hit the ground. The man kicked him several times. He pulled him away from the ambulance and threw him on the pavement. He ignored Tamra's shouts as if he could not hear them. He kicked the man again and left him lying on his stomach. His body shivered and then became still. The Guardian pointed his gun at the man's back and fired several shots. The victim's body shuddered and seemed to jump before it settled down.

'Stop it! For God's sake stop it!' shrieked Tamra.

'Hey take it easy sister. He's only a dirty little Palestinian. Don't upset yourself over him. Come on everybody, bring the other shits out.'

Tamra ran back to her ambulance and stood in front of the doors. Her arms spread out and her face was defiant.

'Sister. Sister, you're upsetting yourself over nothing. Just leave them with us. We'll wait till you've gone. That way you won't see anything. Anybody would think that you knew the motherfuckers!'

'I do,' shouted Tamra.

'You knew him?' asked the Guardian in disbelief.

'Yes. I've known him all my life.'

'Sorry sister. You should've told us. Who was he?'

'His name was Jesus Christ,' she blurted, her anger and fear rising to the pitch of tears.

The Guardians looked at each other uncomprehending for a short while. The killer nodded his head several times.

'All right sister. Take'em and go. Go!! We aren't in the business of upsetting our women . . . Go!' he screeched angrily.

Tamra slammed the doors shut and jumped into the ambulance. As she turned the corner she felt herself shake. She burst out crying. She cried all the way to the Green Line where she handed over her two remaining passengers.

* * *

The Beirut Lunatic Asylum perched on the side of a mountain overlooking the city. Its inmates spent several hours a day looking down on Beirut in bewilderment. During the nights; several of them sat on a large balcony watching the city burn and now and then a few of them would clap their hands in delight at a particularly spectacular explosion or fire.

Amongst the inmates were well known artists, politicians and men of history. One such man was President Nasser who sat on the edge of the balcony analysing the events going on in Beirut. Now and then he would slip back into his old sane self. At these times he would call the nurses and other inmates 'mon enfant' and tell them about the attack on his house.

'Ah mon enfant, they came in the night. We were still asleep. The President always got up very early. We were asleep. Mes enfants, they burst into the house, cut my son's throat and threw me out of the window. But President Nasser could never fly. They had my wife, cut her breasts off and left her to die. I wasn't too angry. That's war mes enfants. But they burned my manuscript . . . I was livid. I ordered my army to find them and retrieve my notes. Hence the fighting in Beirut . . . Mes enfants . . ' He would often cry at this juncture and fall silent for days.

Early one afternoon, the inmates were on the balcony.

Their numbers had swelled dramatically since the beginning of the war. Families who could otherwise look after their mildly mad and harmless members had put them into this haven for the duration of the war. Beirut was very quiet and the air was hot and humid. The President sat in his usual place. Now and then he threw out a few sentences explaining his response to Britain's attack on the Suez.

Suddenly there was gunfire in the highway just outside the asylum. Several nurses came running out and herded the inmates into the ground floor. Many were in a state of panic and crying. Nurses held on to the more frightened patients and tried to calm them down.

The gunfire became very intense and got nearer and nearer to the building. It stopped as suddenly as it had started.

Several gunmen and women burst into the hall where the inmates were kept. One of them opened fire and hit the ceiling.

'Come on everybody. You can go . . .' he shouted to the inmates. Nurses and doctors tried to haggle with the gunmen.

'I said they can go . . .' he repeated shooting into the ceiling again.

One doctor came forward.

'Listen. These people can't fend for themselves out there. For God's sake leave them in here where they can be looked after properly.'

'Look my friend,' shouted one of the women. 'Look. Outside it's a mad world. It should just suit them fine.' Several gunmen started laughing. Some inmates joined in and laughed loudly clapping their hands.

The attackers started herding the inmates out onto the highway. They pointed them towards Beirut laughing and joking all the time. The lunatics started their long haul into Beirut. Some were dancing, others arguing, a few crying.

As the attackers drove off, several of the doctors and nurses drove out to look for their patients. The majority had disappeared and could not be found. A few came back and others were picked up sitting beside the road weeping.

The President was joined by two other inmates.

'Please to have you with us. I am President Nasser. And you? Who are you?'

'Je suis Robespierre,' answered the man.

'Ah,' said the President. 'A great Frenchman. Unfortunately we do not speak that august language. Any chance of conversing in Arabic?'

'Yes of course, Mr President.'

'Good! And you may present yourself my good woman,' said the President looking at the pretty young woman walking by his side.

'My name is Alia,' she answered shyly.

'Alia ... Good name, my dear. And what were you doing in the Presidential Palace?'

'Oh just having a little holiday,' she answered jovially.

'Ah! In the guests' wing. Good. Good. Well, this is the plan of action. We are heading for Beirut. I shall attempt to mediate between the factions as I did in '69. We'll soon have an end to all this nonsense.'

'Good,' answered Robespierre. 'We will soon put an end to all this nonsense.'

'I've just said that,' snapped the President.

'Well! No harm in saying it again.'

'Good. We'll soon put an end to all this nonsense,' repeated the President.

* * *

Tamra returned home exhausted and angry. She could not understand what happened with the Guardians. She kept going over it in her mind. The matter of fact way in which they called her 'sister' and apologised for upsetting her; it was so ridiculous considering what was happening in Beirut. She felt disgusted with her countrymen. She was frightened of what was happening to them.

And Leyla? How was Leyla?

She phoned her hospital and was told that Leyla was out treating Karantina victims on the beaches. Tamra felt a horror at the thought that she had delivered some of those victims into Leyla's arms. If only she could be with her now. Leyla was saner than most. She went about her duty without fuss. Quietly and efficiently as if tomorrow were hers. Probably tomorrow did belong to people like Leyla.

At midnight the telephone rang. It was her father. He wanted her to come to the Green Line where he was stationed for the night. He sounded desperate. Sick with fear and anguish.

She drove at great speed with her sirens blaring. There were not many cars in the streets. Yet the siren allowed her through the checkpoints without much delay.

Her father was waiting for her. He had been crying. His eyes were red and inflamed. She had never seen her father in that state. They went into an adjoining building together.

'Father, what is it?'

He looked at her. He tried to smile but failed as his face was contorted into a look of extreme anguish.

'They've just launched an attack on Damour. They're going in. Revenge for Karantina they call it.'

'Have you been in touch?'

'I can't. The lines are difficult to get. I'm still trying.'

Father and daughter spent the night by the telephone trying the number every few mintues. By five in the morning they managed to get through.

'Who is that?' shouted Pierre. 'Who is it? Can I speak to Mrs Shami? Marie Shami?'

Tamra stood by him. He looked up at her and smiled.

'They're calling her,' he said cheerfully.

'Hello Marie? Hello darling. It's me Pierre. How are things? What's happening? Can you get out? . . .'

'Let me speak to her dad . . .'

Pierre listened to his wife at the other end and his eyes filled with tears. 'No we're all right, my love. We're all right. Tamra is here with me . . .'

He handed the phone to Tamra.

'She wants to talk to you.'

'Hello mummy. How are you?'

'Tamra darling listen to me because I don't have much time. They are already here. You must be able to hear the firing in the background. They've shot a few people. They're loading the others into lorries and driving them out to Beirut. I must go now. I'll see you later. In case I don't . . .'

'Mum!'

'Tamra, you have to be strong. You have to help me. Don't start crying on me now . . .' she added trying to sound jovial. 'Come on Tamra. I want you to look after yourself and after your father. Please look after Pierre. You don't know what this could do to him.'

'We will be all right mum. You just look after yourself and get back here soon. Quick. We miss you. Daddy even misses your cooking . . .' Tamra tried to laugh.

'Good God! Things must be getting bad!!' Marie laughed.

There was a slight silence punctuated by the line crackling. 'Must go now darling. Kiss daddy for me. I'll see you soon. Bye bye love.' The line went dead. Tamra replaced the receiver and turned to her father. He held her to him and patted her head as his body shook with sobs.

* * *

Leyla ran from beach to beach administering to the injured and distressed as best she could. Many were in a state of shock after what they had witnessed in the shantytown. The place buzzed with horror stories that people told each other to relieve their burdened minds.

'They're bulldozing everything,' said one.

'Every little house. They say they're going to have a big beautiful park in its place.'

'Well you can't say my home was worthless. They're turning it into a beautiful park,' said someone jovially. Several people laughed.

Leyla wondered if Tamra had driven any of these people to the Green Line. She could not quite accept that Tamra would have been part of what happened in Karantina. No one she knew could be. Yet she knew Paul and he was fighting on the Phalangists' side. She had had occasion to phone him a few times in an attempt to trace people who had been kidnapped. He had always been very polite and given her what she needed. She even met him once on the Green Line. He had brought a Lebanese Moslem who had been mistaken for a Palestinian and handed him over to one of her colleagues. She had waved at him discreetly from her side of the line. He had nodded and walked away.

She knew that she would have a busy few days ahead trying to have Karantina prisoners released. The negotiations would be very polite and amongst friends since several of the fighters on both sides knew each other and had grown up together.

Leyla did not have it in her heart to hate anyone. Apart from anything else she was constantly busy dealing with arrivals into the hospital. At night, when she did get a chance to go to bed for a short while, her mind was full of passions that she found hard to deal with. She thought of the old days – they seemed so far away. Days of peace and quiet university studies.

These days were gone. They were gone forever it seemed to her. Forever.

Forever.

* * *

Tamra and Pierre sat waiting for news from Damour. As soon as they returned home they heard that the small town had fallen to the Palestinian forces. Its inhabitants were being herded on to the backs of lorries and driven on to

Beirut. Their houses were demolished and put to the torch. There was little left of the small agrarian town that had lived in peace for so long.

At midnight of the next day Paul arrived and was made welcome by Pierre. Tamra saw the two men sitting side by side in their dirty uniforms chatting quietly. She made them some bitter coffee and sat with them. Now and then Paul looked at her and she understood what his eyes were saying.

'Monsieur Pierre,' he started.

'Call me Pierre, son. These days we can dispense with little politenesses, can't we?' smiled Pierre.

'Pierre. I have something to tell you . . ' Paul hesitated. There was a short silence.

The silence was suddenly broken by a long husky roar that came from Pierre. He held his head in his hands and started to sob.

Paul put his hand on Pierre's shoulder and squeezed.

'Pierre. Pierre.'

Tamra got up and sat beside her father. They both cried.

Paul turned to leave them to grieve in private.

'Wait! Don't go!' shouted Pierre.

Paul stood by the door with his hand on the handle.

'What happened?'

'Pierre my friend . . .'

'Answer me! What happened?' said Pierre as quietly as he could.

'They took a little girl away. Marie tried to get her back. She argued with the gunmen to let the girl go. They took her away saying they weren't going to hurt the girl. They were just holding hostages in order to get back some of their own Karantina ones. They wouldn't let Marie take the girl away. She refused to go without her. They removed them both.'

'Then?' faltered Pierre.

'We found them on the airport road, Pierre.'

'Dead?'

'Yes.'

'Had she been . . .?' Pierre stood up.

'Pierre listen to me . . .'

'Had she been touched? Answer my question.'

'Yes. Both of them. The little girl and Marie.'

Pierre walked across the room and stared out of the window. Tamra sat in her place still sobbing quietly.

'As God is my witness,' started Pierre. 'As God is my witness. There will not be one of the motherfuckers left in Lebanon. I'll castrate every son of a bitch of them. Every bastard I can get my hands on. As God is my witness.'

He turned and looked at Paul and Tamra. His face was contorted with hate and vengeance. There was no grief there. Just a will to vengeance.

FIVE

The battle started early in the mountains. It had been raining hard all night. The early morning sky was cloudy, darkened, and gritty. Everything seemed dull, grey and dark. All soil was mud. All roads became running streams churning up mud and dirt along their brown route.

No one knew exactly what started the shooting that morning. Most of Beirut was beginning to wake up when one explosion after another shook many buildings and made people jump up and listen attentively to determine where the firing was coming from.

Near the Green Line, dividing Beirut in two, there lay three bodies with their throats cut. No one knew who they were or how they came to be there. Each side assumed that they belonged to them. Each side had started firing in anger.

Leyla came out of the university campus and hailed a car.

'Is it all right to drive out to Sabra?'

'Yes, dear sister. Jump in. No problem. The seaside road is as calm as it is here. Let's go.'

There were two other passengers in the car. One man sat in the front talking to the driver. In the back sat Leyla and an attractive middle-aged woman. The car raced towards the seafront. Its passengers could hear firing coming mainly from the city centre.

As the car emerged on the seaside route the driver slowed down.

'What is it?' asked the man sitting in the front.

'Road barrier my friend. Come on. Get your papers out.'

He inched his car towards the gunmen standing in the middle of the road. They were obviously Moslem gunmen sporting thick beards and wearing golden Korans around their necks.

As the car came to a halt; Leyla saw two bodies lying on the pavement behind the gunmen.

'Papers!' snapped one of the gunmen putting his gun through the car window.

The driver smiled nervously and handed him the identity cards collected from his passengers.

The gunman looked at the cards one by one. Now and then he would look up and check on the car occupants. His face hardened as he looked up again first at Leyla and then at the woman beside her.

'You!' he shouted looking at her.

The woman was looking out of the other window. She carried on looking away at if he was not addressing her.

'You! Miss Khoury! I'm talking to you!'

The woman turned around and looked at him. Her face was pale. Her eyes were wide with shock and her nostrils flared with terror.

'Get out of the car please.' He sounded almost polite.

The woman opened her door slowly and stepped out of the car. The driver looked around helplessly.

'Anything wrong with her papers my friend?' he asked nervously.

The gunman looked at him for a few seconds. 'Drive away. Come on! Off you go!'

The driver put the car in gear and started off at great speed. Leyla looked back and saw the woman being led towards the two bodies on the pavement. As she tried to step around them she crossed herself several times.

'Stop! Stop!' screeched Leyla.

The driver slammed on his brakes.

'What is it? What is it?'

'I want to get out. Wait for us here.'

'Wait? For us?' said the driver petrified. 'Look sister. You're not going back to those men, are you?'

'Yes. Please wait here. I'll try to bring her back with me.'

'You can't. She's a Christian. They're going to shoot her. Even God Almighty can't save her now. Don't go back!!'

Leyla jumped out of the car and ran back to the checkpoint. She looked over her shoulder shouting to the driver. 'You wait. Just wait there.'

She ran as fast as she could. As she approached the checkpoint, she saw the woman pushed against a low wall behind the two bodies. Two gunmen were walking away from her.

'Stop!! Please stop!'

The gunmen lowered their guns and looked around. Their faces became an absolute comic picture of amazement at the sight of Leyla.

'Please stop. Please brothers.'

'What is it sister? What do you want?' asked the man who had looked at the identity cards.

'Please listen to me for just one minute before you do anything. Please. In the name of the Prophet God's Blessings be upon Him.'

The gunmen respectfully lowered their guns and stepped back. The first speaker walked towards Leyla and escorted her away from the others. He leant against the low wall and looked intently at her.

'Cigarette?' he offered.

'Yes. Thank you,' said Leyla taking one although she had never smoked before.

He inhaled his first few puffs while staring at Leyla clumsily sucking on her cigarette and screwing up her eyes.

'You're not a smoker, are you sister? I've got some real stuff in the car you know. Purest hashish from Baalbeck. Care to try some?'

'Not now. May be some other time though . . .'

The man smiled. 'So we could perhaps see each other again sister?'

'I don't see why not . . .'

'Where do you live then?'

'Bourj el-Barajneh,' lied Leyla her face flushing horribly.

The gunman looked at her red face, smiled, and stroked her cheek. His hand moved down and clutched one of her breasts.

'You're coy. I like that in a woman. Good,' he said with authority. 'What do you want from me in return?' he added abruptly.

'That poor woman,' whispered Leyla.

'Do you know her?'

'No.'

'And you're willing to give me what I want in return for a woman you don't even know. Some fucking shit of a Christian who deserves to have her tits chopped off?' As he spoke he squeezed Leyla's breast into a ruthless pinch that brought tears to her eyes.

'Are you willing to do all that?'

'Yes,' flushed Leyla again.

'Why? Do you know what her people are doing this very second? Do you know what they've been doing all morning? They have set up road blocks everywhere. They're stopping cars and taking out all Moslem passengers and shooting them, whoever they may be. They've killed at least three hundred people since early this morning. They've cut breasts off and left the women in agony on the pavements. I've seen it. I've just seen it at the hospital. Women without breasts lying in corridors like meat at the butcher's. And you really expect me to let this fucking bitch go?'

Leyla was frightened. She realised that she could not really argue with this mentality. His fury and bitterness were all that maintained him at that moment.

'But she is not responsible for what her people have done,' she faltered helplessly.

The man seemed to ignore her for a while as he stared out to sea. Leyla looked at him without daring to say a word.

'Why should I bother to give her to you?' he asked still staring out to sea. His hand moved up to Leyla's face and stroked her hair.

'What for? I could get out of her what you've promised me and then kill her! They're all fucking whores with cunts itching to be filled . . . I'll shoot her just as I am about to . . .'

'Stop it!' shouted Leyla. 'Stop it!' She buried her face in her hands and started to sob.

The gunman suddenly shook himself like someone just woken up. He put an arm around Leyla and patted her shoulder gently.

'There! There! Sister. Don't cry. I'm not going to upset you. Come love. You can take the woman and go. Come. Take her.'

He gently led Leyla to the woman. He pointed the trembling creature towards the spot where the car was still waiting at a distance. He walked them both to the car and gently pushed them in. He patted Leyla's shoulder and his eyes met hers for a split second as he closed the door. She tried to smile but failed, only producing a distant grimace and a gentle tremble. He nodded as if her smile was understood.

As the car moved off, he walked back towards his men.

'Hey! Muhammad! We're wanted in the hotel area. Let's move out!'

Muhammad looked back at the car again before he turned around and ran towards his men.

'Let's go! Come on!' he shouted as he jumped into his jeep.

Down the road the cab driver kept asking Leyla how she had managed to save the woman's life. The woman herself sat impassively staring out of the window. Now and then she squeezed Leyla's hand.

* * *

Muhammad and his men arrived at their destination very soon afterwards. The hotel was a raging battle zone. Several tall buildings were spewing out flames and thick, black smoke. Muhammad's orders were to recapture the Holiday Inn Hotel in hand to hand fighting. From the fifth floor upwards several Christian militiamen were entrenched in a position of firing supremacy. Muhammad and four of his men started to walk up the service stairs and to check the hotel floor by floor. As they walked around the first floor they found several bodies lying aroung or leaning against the walls. Some had been decapitated, other were naked. One woman was slumped over the balcony fully naked with several stab wounds in her back and spine. On overturned furniture lay syringes, packets of cigarettes, silver foil and other evidence of the state of mind of many of the fighting men and women.

One of Muhammad's men leant against a wall and vomited clutching his stomach.

'All right everybody. Let's stop a little. Here lad, take this,' he said passing a cigarette to the sick man. 'The best Lebanese shit that money can buy. Straight from Baalbeck to your blood stream!' he added jovially.

The sick man sank against the wall and smoked deep and long. He held his breath after each deep inhalation. His face relaxed as his eyes seemed to water slightly. His head nodded forward and he seemed to fall asleep for a few seconds.

'Come on! We've got a job to do!'

The men gingerly inched their way upstairs. Muhammad led them to the fifth floor. They could hear men and women laughing amidst countless explosions. Muhammad motioned his men to stop where they were as he crouched and started to shift his body forward.

As he reached the fifth floor fire exit he could see that there was one man standing against the wall smoking hashish whilst his friends were obviously in the room in front of him. It was from that room that the firing and laughter were coming. Muhammad returned to his group.

'Right! Listen! There's a shit stoned out of his wits guarding the room. I'll get the bastard without any noise. As soon as he is gone; you move in. Shoot to kill. Don't leave a single one of the murdering bastards.'

They moved up the stairs again. Muhammad went in first and quickly moved up to the man who was just lighting another cigarette. There was a distant gurgling sound and the man fell forward with his throat bleeding and smoke floating out of the wound. As his men moved forward; Muhammad's hand went up and down plunging the knife into the quivering body.

The shooting only lasted a few seconds. Of the eight Christians in the room three died instantly. Two were injured, and one ran towards the balcony and went flying over the edge. His screams were the last that could be heard as the firing stopped.

Muhammad walked into the room and looked at the two injured and two prisoners – a man and a woman. One of the prisoners smiled at him while the other kept laughing. His men started to laugh with them too. The laughing woman came forward and put her arm out as if to shake hands.

'Come on boys! Let's have fun!' shouted someone.

The woman was grabbed by two men who started to undress here while at the same time beating her. She did not resist although she carried on laughing and crying at the same time.

'What about the other bastards?' shouted one of the men. Muhammad did not answer him. He walked out of the room and stood near the fire exit lighting a cigarette.

'Put them on the bannister outside. And push one of them off as I start to spunk in this fucking whore. Hold her down. Spread 'em out you fucking bitch . . .'

Muhammad wondered if he would ever see that beautiful woman again. Her beauty in the middle of all this. It did not fit. She did not fit amidst the screams of the woman that he could hear at that very second. Yet that was exactly what he would have liked to do with her. He had felt that uncontrollable urgency burning within his loins. An urgency that was born of war. Of untamed savagery and total indifference. He had forgotten to ask her what her name was. He had seen it in her identity card. He could not remember it. She did not fit amidst all this filth and squalor. This was cruelty beyond his old innocence. His men must stop. He must make them stop. Grass or no grass. Nothing could justify this kind of cruelty. They must stop. Now.

He turned around to walk back to his men. He was faced by a man he had never seen before.

'In the name of the Virgin Mary!' said the man as he put a hand on Muhammad's mouth and slammed a wide knife into his ribs.

The man stepped back.

Muhammad reeled a few seconds. His arm stretched towards the man as if he wanted to say something to him. He slid against the wall moving down slowly with a distant smile on his face.

'The bastard's smiling!' exclaimed someone.

'Stoned out of his wits, the Moslem shit.'

'What about the others?'

'We've got them. All dead except one. They've fucked Mary.'

Muhammad's vision was beginning to blur. He thought about the beautiful woman who had saved his prisoner's life. He saw her standing in front of him. She knelt before him and smiled. She was naked and he could not understand why. Had she come to pay off her debt? She had promised him that he could have her. Her hand came out and stroked his cheek. He tried to lift his hand to touch her firm breasts. She looked down at them and smiled at him encouragingly.

He heard her whisper something. 'Don't be frightened. All's going to be all right . . .'

He tried to smile at her.

'Phillipe! Phillipe!' she whined looking intently at Muhammad. 'Spunk in me while they turf this shit off the balcony. Please Phillipe. Please!'

Muhammad smiled again at Leyla. Leyla. That was her name.

His head slumped forward.

* * *

Tamra got out of the car outside the huge villa grounds. A smartly uniformed man saluted as he held doors open for her. In the distance could be heard continuous thundering explosions and the crackling of gunfire.

Tamra had been invited to a soirée at a family friend's villa on the beach in an attempt to help her get over her mother's death. The friend came forward beaming gracefully.

'Oh how lovely to see you. I hope your drive was not too difficult. These awful battles are such a nuisance. How are you? If you grow any more beautiful we older women shall have to watch out for our husbands!'

Tamra, feeling intensely ill at ease at having accepted to go out to a soirée during the fighting, tried to smile politely and said nothing. The two joined the other guests on the long balcony where a sumptuous table had been laid. All took their seats as the hostess explained that she had had to change the venue for their dinner.

'I do hope you don't mind the covered balcony my dears. But I thought that it would be a great pity to miss that lovely sunset and other views . . .' she added embarrassedly. In the background the sky was alight with unextinguished fires in the hotel area and the burning old city centre.

The conversation generally hovered on the sidelines of the war. Now and then someone would mention a new film or a new book. Everyone would listen politely and then return to the business of war.

Tamra walked around the balcony feeling intensely

ashamed. She simply could not believe that anyone would want to dress up and have a private dinner party when their city burnt before their very eyes. She felt angry. Yet she could understand why they were doing it. This was one of the ways of surviving the misery of war. Continue playing as normal and the war can not touch you. And it was done to please her. She wished that she had not come.

Suddenly voices were raised amongst the male guests. Tamra looked around and saw several of them shouting and waving their arms about. The wives were trying to calm their husbands down.

'Are you telling me that our men actually take that sort of stuff in order to find the courage to fight?'

'I am!'

'How dare you? They're good Maronites. They don't need drugs to get them going. It's only those Moslem shits who take that stuff . . .'

'Now, now, my dear. There really is no need to swear at the dinner table. Would you like a drink, love?'

The man ignored his wife and continued to stare at his opponent. The latter sat back, lit a cigar, and puffed contentedly like someone who had done well in a crossword puzzle against the greatest odds.

'But they do,' said Tamra.

The silence that followed Tamra's declaration was electric. No one dared speak.

Her hostess looked at her and smiled. 'What did you say, my dear?'

'I said that they do. The fighters do take drugs. They do it on both sides. It's nothing to do with religion. They just do it. Otherwise how do you think that they can do what they do to each other. They must be taking something. If they're not then the whole of Lebanon is even madder than I thought. No sane person can do what they do to each other and not be mad or on drugs.'

The long silence was again broken by the mortified hostess. She laughed and walked up to Tamra.

'My dear, we really are going to look out for our husbands! You're something else, my dear.'

And she walked Tamra back to the table where everyone was smiling and trying to forget whether the Lebanese were on drugs or just mad.

* * *

Paul received word to go to the Phalangist headquarters in Ashrafiyeh as quickly as possible. He left Jounieh, where his unit was stationed, and drove at great speed. He had to stop at several checkpoints before being waved on towards East Beirut.

At the headquarters he was swiftly ushered upstairs where he was met by the party's Chief Security Officer.

'Paul! Thank God you're here. Sit down. Sit down.' The Security Officer seemed both nervous and excited. 'Would you like a coffee?'

'No thanks. What is it? What's the matter? Where's Beshir?'

'Beshir's gone down to the hotel area. He wants you to join your men there as soon as possible.'

'What's going on? Have we lost?'

'No. And we haven't won either. My God Paul. It's unbelievable down there. We're fighting hand to hand from hotel floor to hotel floor. We take one floor then they take it away from us. We've got to the ridiculous position of having alternate floors at the Holiday Inn. And each side is committing the most horrendous atrocities . . .' The Officer wiped his forehead and got up. He walked towards the window and stood there looking out.

'Paul! They're screwing half dead prisoners and killing 'em as they orgasm. Half of the sods are on drugs. They're stoned out of their frigging minds.'

'What did you expect?' asked Paul. 'This is no picnic. You send men into street hand to hand fighting over and over again. What do you expect them to do? Waltz with each other? They're bound to crack?'

'Yes! Yes! I know Paul. But this is a war in which we are trying to safeguard our territory. We have to make certain moves to maintain our own safety. The hotel area is important to us. But this has turned into one massive and terrifying orgy of rape and massacres . . .'

Paul got out of his chair and went to the officer. He put his hand on his shoulder and said, 'Don't worry. We will try to stop this if we can.'

'Thanks Paul . . . I want every bastard who's found drugged shot on the spot!'

Paul arrived at the hotel area with his force of selected men and women. He immediately set about to retake the Holiday Inn. In virtually no time, his men had taken several floors of the hotel and were arresting anyone of their own side who happened to be on drugs. Men, singing and laughing, were herded into cars and driven out at great speed as the new force started to build up its fortification in preparation for a long defence of their little enclave.

The counter attack was not long in coming. Paul, standing on the eleventh floor, could see long convoys of Palestinians moving towards the area. It was difficult to judge how many there were or whether they were all Palestinians. It was not long before news reached him that the Palestinian forces were also joined by Lebanese army units and other Lebanese Moslem factions. Paul knew that all was lost. There was no way in which his men could hold out against such a massive force.

They deployed themselves as best they could. Several stood on balconies hurling grenades at the attacking forces. As the attackers took the hotel floor by floor, Paul and his men would retreat to the next storey.

After a fierce battle lasting the whole day, Paul and the remaining survivors asked to be allowed to surrender. There were only three of them left. One was injured in the shoulder and sat against the wall crying.

Ironically, thought Paul, they were sent there to clean up their own operation!

Several of the victors stormed into the room and started kicking their prisoners. The wounded man was hauled high above their heads and hurled out of the window his screams dying as he shot down the twenty-six floors.

Paul and his companion were half dragged and half walked down the stairs. In the hotel lobby they were pushed against the wall while the victors jubilated and had photographs taken of themselves. In front of them lay the headless corpse of one of Paul's men.

'Come on boys. Let's show West Beirut what we've got us today!'

Several bodies were tied to the victors' jeeps and dragged around the neighbourhood amidst the clapping, singing, and shooting of their captors. Both Paul and his companion were stood on the first floor balcony to watch this.

'Take a good look my friend. That's what's going to happen to you! Remember Karantina you fucking bastards?! Just watch this and you'll know what we're going to do to your people. You murdered ours. Now it's you're fucking turn. Watch. Watch the little shits being dragged around. They're luckier than you. At least they're dead.'

'Hey You!!' shouted a familiar voice from behind them. The guards turned around and saluted smartly at the sight of the Palestinian Military Police.

'How dare you?' the commander screeched. 'What kind of behaviour is this? Is this the way that we treat our enemy?'

The five guards looked sheepishly around them. Paul's heart jumped when he recognised his party's Security Officer standing before them in a Palestinian uniform.

'Come on. Move it. Get moving . . . We'll take the prisoners.'

The guards turned around and started to walk down the stairs. No sooner had they moved than the Security Officer and his men opened fire. The Palestinians shot forward, their screams of horror and surprise mingling with crackling firing.

'Come on,' he shouted. 'Let's get out of here. There's no way we can hold this place. Let's move.'

Paul followed his saviours as they rushed out of the hotel into two armoured cars belonging to the Palestine Command and raced into East Beirut.

'Here Paul,' said the Officer giving him a cigarette.

'How are things in the mountains?'

'Bad. Very Bad. We're losing. Even Bikfaya is threatened. We're losing Paul. Losing to those fucking Palestinians and their Moslem allies. Bastards!'

'Hey chief, listen. It's Pierre Gemayel,' shouted the driver turning his radio up.

Gemayel's voice was steady but tired. He spoke solemnly.

'Our people and our army are dispersed, our institutions are disintegrating and our land occupied. There is no legislature, no judiciary, no sovereignty, no security and no freedom. Ruin and destruction spread over villages and cities, towns and mountains. I appeal to you all, men and women, to unite for the homeland. Perform your holy duty of defending the homeland which faces disintegration.'

The driver switched the radio off. The two armoured cars continued their journey eastwards. Paul and his companions fell into a deep and morose silence.

* * *

As the Christian forces started to retreat everywhere, they unleashed salvo after salvo of aimless barrages of bombardment against their Moslem and Palestinian enemies. Rocket propelled grenades, rockets, tracers swept over the Beirut skyline landing in civilian areas near the seafront.

Leyla worked almost non-stop helping the injured and the dying into various makeshift hospitals. Several of her helpers were cheerful as they saw their side winning the war. One badly injured colleague smiled at her saying, 'And we're supposed to be winning! Shit! What would it be like if we started to lose?' Leyla laughed and helped him into the nearest available car.

Late in the night Muhammad Salman came in search of his daughter. Her mother was worried since neither she nor Imad had been in touch for days.

'But father, you can see what we have to do here? We're up to our neck in this. That's why I haven't been home. Tell mum not to worry. We'll be all right. We're needed here. That's all. She mustn't worry.'

'Listen Leyla. Since Rashid left us, your mother has been very worried about you children. Do me a favour. As soon as you're able to, would you find Imad and ask him to visit home when he can. I know what it's like here for both of you. But do try and see your poor mother.'

'Yes father. I'll find him. And we'll come in as soon as we can. I promise.'

By the end of the next day, Leyla was told to go home and rest for a while. She left immediately and went in search of Imad. She had been told that he was last seen near the American Embassy at the seafront helping the wounded who had escaped from the battle of the hotels.

She borrowed one of her peoples' cars and drove towards the Embassy. The evening air was cool and bracing. It had been raining most of the day. The smell was fresh tinged with that slight saltiness that can only be experienced on the Beirut seafront.

Leyla parked her car near the American Embassy. As she stepped out of it an explosion shook the neighbourhood and she threw herself to the ground. Several cars on the other side of the road burst into flames. Five or six American marines guarding the Embassy rushed and tried to put the fires out. Leyla got up and ran away towards the entrance to the hotel area. There she found several ambulances lined up beside armoured cars. Imad was leaning against one of the ambulances looking pale and frightened.

'God! Imad! What is it?'

Imad looked at his sister for a while and then turned his head away.

'Oh God! You can't imagine what's going on in there. It's unbelievable. It's horrifying. They're mad. They must be sick!'

Leyla nodded several times and took her brother's hand.

'Can you leave now?'

'I suppose so. Nobody's going to be particularly bothered . . .' Imad's lips trembled as he tried desperately to control his feelings.

'Come on love. Let's go home. Come on.'

Brother and sister walked away hand in hand towards Leyla's borrowed car. Several American marines stood beside it chatting to Lebanese Security Forces and watching the cars burn themselves out.

'Where're you two going?' asked a police officer.

'Sabra,' answered Leyla.

'Papers!!' he snapped.

Leyla and Imad produced their blue refugee cards and handed them over. The policeman looked at them. He returned the cards as he spat a white globule at a great distance.

'Who are they?' asked a marine.

'A couple of Palestinian terrorists,' snapped the Lebanese officer.

'Yuh. Yuh.' agreed the marine smiling.

Imad made a sudden movement forward. Leyla had her hand firmly locked around his as she dragged him back away from the officers and the marines.

As they turned the corner, Imad started to shake. She tried to pretend that she could not see him.

'Sorry sister. Sorry.'

'Nothing to be sorry for love,' she answered gently.

'Oh yes there is. There is. Did you hear what that bastard just called us? I've spent the last two days patching many of his own people up. My God! You can't believe what they've been doing to each other in that place. If

Lebanon wants a day to celebrate the point of no return in its self-destruction today would do very well. Rape. Murder. Torture. Sick, sick behavior. You've never seen anything like it. Anything. And then we have to come out here and hand over our blue cards. My God! The arrogant bastards!'

'Imad. We can't go on hating like this. We really can't. It is this kind of hatred that's keeping this war going. We must try not to hate like this.'

'Leyla. Leyla. You haven't seen what they've done back there. You haven't seen them dragging live men hitched to cars. You haven't seen men with their penises in their mouths. You haven't . . .'

'Yes. Yes. I know love.' Leyla touched Imad's hand and squeezed it as they headed for their parents' small home.

* * *

'It's ironic, isn't it?' asked Paul.

'What is my friend?' asked the Security Officer as the two men sat together in the latter's office.

'It's ironic that we are saved from a crushing defeat at the hands of the Palestinians by the interference of our worst enemy: the Syrians.'

'Perhaps. Though I don't really think so. I would be happy to have made an alliance with the devil himself to save Lebanon from those people.'

'Yes. But who's going to get rid of the Syrians when they've served their purpose?'

'We will. It wouldn't be the first time we had a foreign enemy with designs on us. And it wouldn't be the first time we've managed to kick them out. Especially those fucking barbarians the Syrians. And if we can't get them out. Why then we'll ally ourselves with the Israelis who would get them out in less than five minutes. No. Sorry. Got that wrong. It was five minutes in sixty-seven. I mean six seconds.' The Officer seemed highly amused by his analysis of the situation and laughed heartily at the projected discomfiture of the Syrians.

'I'm not so sure,' said Paul almost thinking out loud and talking to himself. 'I'm not so sure that it's going to work. We'll have peace for a while and then we'll start again. It's not over. I saw what happened at the battle for the hotels. People who could do such things to each other are not going to forget for a long time.'

'Oh come on Paul. Don't be so damned sensitive. Those people were stoned out of their tiny little minds. That's why they did these things. It'll all be forgotten in a few weeks. Wait and see.'

'I don't think that people will forget. The killers may have been drugged but the victims weren't. These things won't – can't – be forgotten.'

'Well Paul! For a philosopher you've certainly fallen down on this little argument. Listen to me. If the killers were drugged then they won't remember. If the victims weren't drugged then by virtue that they were victims they would be dead and would therefore not remember either. Ergo, everyone will forget. Voilà!!!'

Paul wished that he could be as cheerful as his friend. He could not get himself to forget the things that he had recently seen and heard. He could not get away from the fact that the Syrians had occupied his country even if it meant saving the Christian community. He could not accept the introduction of more foreign elements into the Lebanese quagmire.

This war could not yet be over. When, he thought, oh when will we rebuild Lebanon? When will we all live in harmony?

As he asked himself this question, he realised for the first time that he had included other people in his 'we'. This 'we' included all Lebanese regardless of religion or race. Everyone and forever.

Forever.

SIX

The journey into Israel was a matter of minutes by helicopter. Yet blindfolded, Rashid felt as if it took ages. His helplessness made things worse. He did not know where he was being taken and what was to become of him. Around him he could hear the engine with the distant voices of men talking in an efficient pointed manner.

The helicopter landed. He was bundled out by a man who spoke excellent Arabic and who held him by his arm steering him away. It was obviously a sandy area as the ground felt soft beneath his feet. He tried to figure out where he might be. He wondered if he was being taken to one of Israel's notorious camps that he had heard so much about during his training. As yet he had little time to feel any fear or panic.

He was surprised not to hear anyone talking as he and his escort walked together. He could hear his escort's breathing with its gentle whistle appearing every time he inhaled.

The escort's hand on Rashid's arm tightened as he ordered him to stop. He half pushed him and half pulled him as Rashid confusedly tried to follow his captor's instructions.

'Get into the fucking jeep will you?' shouted the man gruffly.

His escort sat beside him and said something in

Hebrew. The engine started and Rashid felt the sudden forward movement of the jeep. The road was bumpy and he was worried by the wind. He was a man floating on air. He did not dare move in his seat for fear of falling off. He wondered how open this jeep was. He sat still and straight.

His instructions were to say nothing. He wondered whether he would be able to maintain silence. How much torture could he take? How many hours without sleep? How many hours without food? What other forms of torture would they use on him? Would they use drugs? What could he tell them anyhow?

All he had to do was to keep denying that he knew anything. He was sent out to seek and destroy. That was all. He was not important within the PLO. He knew no one. He knew nothing. All he had to do was to play stupid. What could he think of to keep himself sane? He could compose poems.

He thought of the little poems he had composed for Tamra. He wondered where she was at that minute. With Leyla perhaps. Yes. He could think of Tamra to keep himself sane. He could concoct a whole new relationship between them in order to survive this. When alone he would talk to her and recite her some poems.

The thought cheered him up a little. His mind returned to the present situation. The jeep was still moving on bumpy ground. His escort had obviously lit a cigarette. Or was it the driver? From the direction of the wind, Rashid tried to work out who was smoking. After careful consideration he decided that it was probably his escort and that he would make a terrible blind man. He wondered what his escort looked like. Was he young? Old? From his voice he sounded young – even carefree. Rashid imagined him to be a tallish fellow with a slight stoop from the way he had held his arm. He probably had thick hair which he kept having to push back from his forehead. Or perhaps glasses that he kept having to push back into place every time they slid down.

Would Tamra remember him? Would she know where he was? How much did Leyla tell her? They were very good friends. They were so close that it almost felt as if Tamra was a member of his family the way Leyla talked about her. But he had only seen her a few times. Those magnificent blue eyes. The colour of the sea. And her long soft hair. And according to Leyla an absolutely brilliant girl. A scientist? She would probably laugh at his poems.

Her voice fascinated him. Very difficult to describe it as anything but ordinary; yet it had a slightly guttural depth to it that made it sound distant and all powerful. It was a full voice. Rashid felt a tinge of excitement at the thought of her talking to him alone. Reading his poems aloud.

'Out! Come on. Let's get moving.'

He had not realised that the jeep had stopped. He felt someone take hold of his legs and swing them over the side. He slid on his bottom and landed on hard rocky ground. His escort took his arm and steered him firmly.

'You're home!' said his escort. 'I'm going to have to leave you my friend. One day we might get better acquainted.'

Rashid was about to say 'thank you' when he checked himself. He was dying to find out what the man looked like. He wanted to ask. But he controlled his urge because to ask would have indicated the weakness of curiosity. It would have shown that blindfolding him was working. It was undermining his faith in his existence. He must keep silent.

'Come on old fellow,' said a kindly female voice. 'This way to your new home.'

Nails dug into his arm and he was led again. He had to use all his concentration to avoid tripping on a changeable rocky surface. Suddenly, the ground beneath became smooth and the air around him was cooler. He knew that he had entered some kind of building. Probably a large one from the way that his escort's footsteps were echoing. He heard a rolling sound and a clang as of large doors closing.

'Stand here!' ordered the escort.

He stood alone waiting. What would happen next? Would they take the blindfold off?

He waited without moving. He eventually decided that he might have to stand there for a long time. He wanted to find out. It was the unknown that was their strongest weapon. The unknown of being blindfolded, of where he was, of what would happen next. All this unknown would break a man. He moved one leg by shuffling slightly.

'Stand still!' came a loud, echoing male voice. 'Don't move a fucking thing! Understand?'

Rashid nodded slowly. So that was it. Blindfolded and statued. Blindfolded and statued. Blindfolded and statued stood I.

Air cooled and alone
lightless.

Before, behind, above:
void.

Beneath: a question
unanswerable.

Where was the woman? Had she also gone? Would he never see her face either?

But I'm a poet, he thought. I wonder if I told them whether things would be all right. Inwardly, he smiled again to think that being a poet would make any difference. But the indignity of torturing an artist as if he were just anybody was too much. His nobility should be his protection.

Blindfolded and statued stood I . . .

He felt the taste of blood in his mouth. The same sort of taste he had after a thoroughly good clean at the dentist's. Blood and dryness.

Bloodfolded and statued. Blindfolded.

How long have I been standing here? Minutes probably. But my mouth is so dry. Had I fallen asleep? Standing up? Is that possible?

Tamra. She would probably be with Leyla now. They might be at the Uncle Sam's drinking coffee. Coffee. Sweet and always lukewarm. Never hot. Yet somehow steaming in the cold of the Beirut winter and the heat of its summer. The food was cheap but delicious. Within it was the very taste of Beirut's steamy winter days. As always, it also had the taste of Beirut's humid summer days.

He felt someone undoing his tied hands. Both hands fell beside him with a surge of pain through both as he regained his feeling in them. He tried to lift one of his hands to his blindfold. He could not do it. His arms fell down almost with a groaning noise. They felt so heavy.

'Take the rest of your things off,' ordered the male voice.

Again Rashid tried to lift his hand to take his vest off. He could not do it. A rough pair of hands pulled the vest off his head and pushed his underwear to the ground. He was pushed sideways to step out of them.

He had completely forgotten that he was down to his underwear all that time. And now he quickly ignored the fact that he was naked.

He felt a hand on his shoulder pushing him down.

'Sit down!'

Rashid sat on what felt like a straw chair that had bits prickling into his buttocks.

His hands seemed to lift themselves and land on his legs which he closed tightly. He wondered what he might look like. Could they see his penis? Incongruently, it struck him as ridiculous modesty to worry about his penis being seen at this stage. Was the woman with the kindly voice still there?

'Now listen carefully my friend because I'm not really in the mood for repeating myself.' This was a new voice. It was the voice of an older man. It seemed to be the voice of someone whose years had taught him to regard kindness as a weakness.

'Now, are you listening to me? I am going to ask you a few questions. They are simple factual questions. And I want simple factual answers. Agreed?'

'I know nothing,' said Rashid. 'I know nothing beyond what I was doing yesterday or whenever it was your people kidnapped me.'

'I'm not going to argue with you about the 'kidnapping' bit. We're all entitled to some dignity. And in your situation the dignity of pretence is the best. So let's have it that we kidnapped you. What were you doing when you were kidnapped?'

'I was walking back to Beirut. I had been home at my parents.'

'Visiting? I see. And where is it that your goodly parents live, my friend?'

'Chamaa,' replied Rashid surprising himself with the speed of his lie and the conviction with which he threw it out. He almost believed himself that he had parents in the small village. It reminded him of the time when, lying as a child, he would work himself into believing his own lies with the accompanying indignation at not being believed.

There was a silence in the room. Rashid strained, trying to listen to what was going on. He could discern movement and whispers at a distance. He realised again that the room must be immense. Maybe it was a hangar. It felt like one.

'My friend. You're lying to me . . . Now wait. Don't argue. Because, my friend, I'll tell you exactly how I know that you're lying to me. Our people know every little person who lives in that part of Lebanon. Pathetic little souls with their guilts written across their foreheads. We know them all. And my friend no parent there has had a visit from any son in the Chamaa area.'

Rashid felt the man's breath very near his face. He got the impression that they were alone. Yet he knew that they could not be alone since the man had obviously consulted with others. Maybe he was receiving orders from somebody.

'Now listen my friend. I'm not in authority here. I'm only doing my job. And my job is to get information out of you. Now I know that you were the man who injured our soldiers. We won't bother to discuss this. Our forensic people could prove it in seconds. But we shan't even bother. I also know that you're from the PLO. I even understand why you did what you did. I just want some information from you about Beaufort and its fortifications and about a few other minor things. Now what do you think? Wouldn't it be easier if you gave me the information half voluntarily? I'm going to get it anyhow. If you don't give it to me than I have to hand you over to my boss. And these people can really get you talking. Now what say you?' The man sounded amicable. So reasonable.

'Piss off! Go fuck your mother!' shouted Rashid. He stiffened awaiting the first blow. But nothing happened. The man came even nearer to his face and whispered, 'Suit yourself my friend. I was only trying to make it easier for you. That's all. Okay boss, he's all yours.'

Rashid heard footsteps walking away from him. He could not hear anyone come near him. Yet he felt a hand land on his shoulder.

'Well old fellow,' said the kindly female voice. 'Well! Well! So you want it the hard way, eh?'

Rashid did not answer. He braced himself for the hard time ahead.

In the dark blackness all about
Sat the prisoner silent and fearsome
Hands crawling . . .

Rashid felt a female hand gently crawl up his leg. It almost floated without touching him.

'Well old fellow. Is this nice? Do you like a woman feeling you like this? You've got a rather nice prick, haven't you? Good hefty balls.'

Rashid tried not to make a noise as her hand started to squeeze. The pain started to sear through his lower abdomen. It seemed to fill his whole stomach and rise to his throat. As the pain spread through his whole body, he let out a very loud roar that he hardly recognised as his own. And still she squeezed and twisted. He fell forward and tried to take her hand away. Something struck him hard across his face and he fell over.

How easy it was to talk about not saying anything. How easy to take refuge in poetry. He tried to lie on the floor and shut his eyes behind the blindfold. He tried to think of Tamra. He wondered if she liked poetry.

Someone lifted him up and put him back on the chair. He felt faint and desperately wanted to be sick.

He kept telling himself that if you go through the first few nasty episodes you could survive the whole thing without breaking down. That was how so many people survived torture. That was how everybody wrote about it.

'Now my dear old fellow. That was only a beginning. Just a beginning. I'm going to make you feel better by putting some soothing cream on it.'

He felt her hands take his penis and rub it gently with cool cream. One hand went beneath and gently rubbed the cream on his testes. The sensitivity was excruciating, yet the cream made things slightly better. He felt something being wrapped around his penis and testes. He gasped.

'You've guessed haven't you old fellow? The jelly helps the electricity through . . .'

Conscious of an inner shame at his indignity, conscious of his acrid fear and his parched mouth; Rashid screamed over and over again in a deep hollow sound as each shock went through him. This felt like hours and hours of agony.

'Oh dear. The old fellow has wet himself. Dear. Dear. Never mind we've caught enough of it to make you drink it when you're really thirsty. Okay old fellow?'

Rashid was full of indignant fury. His was the fury of someone who no longer cared.

'Go fuck your mother you miserable cunt. I'm not saying anything. I've got nothing to say. Nothing!'

'No old fellow. I'm going to fuck you eventually. Would you like that?'

'That's all you're fit for you Jewish whore!!'

Rashid heard several steps run towards him. He fell off

his chair after the first blow. He received an endless number of blows and kicks. He tried to cover his head and the kicks increased. In the background he could hear the kindly female voice shouting. 'For God's sake don't kill him. Don't kill him!'

He thought; at least they want me alive. Whatever happens they're not going to kill me. The bottom line is that I'm getting out of this alive. I'm getting out of this alive. He felt himself go under. He tried to think of Tamra. Tried to call her name over and over again. She gave him comfort.

* * *

As Rashid came round he felt a hand in his with soft, warm breath against his cheek. He could not see anything although he felt that he was in a soft, comfortable bed.

'You'll be all right. Don't move my love,' said a female voice.'

'Tamra?'

'Yes dear.'

He lay back and relaxed. His whole body ached. His head felt heavy. He realised that his eyes were not blindfolded. He could not open them. He tried to lift his hand to his face but could not.

'Don't move. Don't move, darling. You'll be all right.'

'Did I talk Tamra? Did I tell them anything?'

'No my love. Nothing. Not a single word. Go to sleep now Rashid. Go to sleep.'

As Rashid sank into a deep sleep; he wondered how it was that he had Tamra beside him. He wanted to ask her how he got there. Who rescued him? How did they get him out?

He slept.

* * *

Rashid came to and shut his eyes immediately. They felt very sensitive and painful. He opened them again. They stuck together. He could just distinguish the small room that he was in. He tried to move but changed his mind and lay still.

He lay for a long time falling asleep and waking up with little starts. Every time he woke up he would remember that he might still be in Israeli hands. He had to make an effort to forget his dream and face reality. He thought of the times when, as a child, he would wake up in the morning with a heart starting light and getting heavier as he realised that today was another day of school and tests and teachers.

He heard the clanging of a door being unlocked and opened. He tried to sit up but only managed to lift himself on one elbow. A uniformed man walked towards him with a tray in his hands. He nodded and sat beside the bed.

Rashid took the spooned soup like an obedient child. He was conscious of the need to build up his strength. As he ate he looked at the man and wondered whether he was one of his torturers.

'Who are you?' he asked in Arabic. The man ignored him and carried on feeding him. He had a gentle face with receding hair and little pretty freckles on his nose. He looked European.

'Do you speak English?'

'Yes,' whispered the man.

'Where am I?'

'In an Israeli detention camp. Now try to eat some more.'

'But . . .' started Rashid thinking of Tamra and his short conversation with her. He knew that it was not a dream. He had felt her hand on his forehead and he had felt her warm breath against his cheek. It was Tamra. He had not been dreaming. He knew that he had not been dreaming.

He tried to gather his thoughts in order to figure out what had happened to him. What could it be?

Suddenly he panicked: he had obviously talked. He had been drugged and had answered all the questions that he had been asked. He must have. That was how they knew about Tamra. That was how they worked on him. He must have talked.

The man noticed his agitation and looked at him sympathetically.

'Come now. Lie down and try to take some more soup.'

'Who are you?'

'Never mind that now my friend. Just relax. You've been badly beaten. You've several broken bones. Lie still.'

'Did I . . .?' But Rashid could not ask the question that was uppermost in his mind.

'I don't know anything about your interrogation. Why you people have to be such heroes is beyond me. One injection and you start singing like little birds.'

Rashid turned his face to the wall and his eyes filled with tears. The man put his tray down and held his hand.

'Listen my friend. My job is to get you feeling better so that you can join the others in the camp. All this is not going to help. Take it easy and let's work on it together.

Rashid turned around and looked at the sympathetic face. He smiled and his face hurt. The man tapped his hand, picked up his tray and left the room.

For weeks Rashid remained in his small cell recovering from the beating. He saw no one except his sympathetic jailer who gave him his food, water, shaving materials and, after a while, some Arabic books. They talked little and managed to survive well. The books came about by accident when the jailer came in one day with a newspaper in his pocket. It was the Jerusalem Post. Rashid's eyes were riveted onto its front page as it stuck out of the man's pocket. The kindly jailer noticed that look, took the paper out of his pocket, put it on the floor and left the room without it.

The next day he asked Rashid what he liked to read.

'Poetry.'

'No harm in that,' answered the man abruptly.

Eventually the two men talked a little more. Rashid found out that his jailer had originally come from Canada. He described it as an endlessly beautiful country with extremes of everything. But he would not be drawn as to why he had left a place so beautiful to come to a land that at best was constantly threatened with war and destruction.

* * *

Rashid was transferred from his cell to a prison camp five months later. He did not have a chance to say goodbye to the man who had looked after him. He never even found out his name. The man's acts of kindness were very much low key and en passant.

On the morning of Rashid's transfer, the man had brought him his breakfast. Rashid had washed and dressed and eaten. He did not know which part of Israel he was in or in what kind of compound or with how many others like him. The only topics that seemed to be allowed were Canada and Arabic poetry. And even in those cases the men kept themselves to the barest surface statements about the beauty of one and the greatness of the other.

By the time that Rashid was being transferred he had grown to have a very romantic notion of Canada. He saw it as a country where trees grew tall and evergreen and where he could find solitude and poetry in nature. He imagined himself living in one of its massive forests eating off the land and spending most of his time reading and writing. It was a dream that kept him alive as much as Tamra had done before.

Not that he had stopped thinking of her. He thought of her most of all at night when he was unable to sleep. He would talk to her. At times the conversations would be very intimate – even obscene. But it did not matter since it kept him alive. It kept him burning with hope that life was still worthwhile. And the obscenity humanised his position and gave him practical ways of surviving.

Rashid's journey to his new camp was in the dark as he had been blindfolded and his hands had been tied behind his back.

However, his indignity did not last long as the transport took less than an hour.

The camp was made up of several huts and tents in which sat, lay, or squatted hundreds of Palestinians. The rules were obviously very strict since no one seemed to be moving about the grounds although it was the middle of the afternoon. Rashid was marched to a small hut where he was told to go in and wait till they were called out.

As he sat on a small mattress he got his eyes accustomed to the comparatively dark room. He noticed several other men squatting or sitting around. They were all dressed in blue, as he was, sported thick beards, which he did not.

A man beside him offered him a cigarette. He took it although he was indifferent. It was only the thought of being able to choose that attracted him. He smiled at the man.

The man smiled and nodded.

'Could be worse, brother. Could be worse.'

And it suddenly struck Rashid that he could be sitting in this gloomy little hut for years and that it could not really be worse.

He thought of Tamra and of Canada.

SEVEN

'Mr President, shall I undress?' asked Alia quietly. The three were sitting in a small pine forest. The grass around them was scorched dry and the night air was full of humidity.

'Mr President, shall I undress?' asked Alia again.

'Yes my girl. Yes. I have not had my wife for some time.'

'But she's not your fucking wife!' shouted Robespierre.

'How dare you?' bellowed the President. 'Apologize at once. I demand an apology.'

'Sorry Mr President,' said Robespierre sheepishly.

'Good man. No harm will come to you. You may have her after me my good man.'

The woman disappeared behind a few trees followed by the President. Robespierre sat in his place gathering pine needles in his hand and squeezing them. He would then open his hand and let go of them and laugh at the ones that stuck into his palm. He would spend some time picking them out one by one and throwing them before him. He repeated this process all the time that the other two were behind the tree. He could hear them clearly.

'You are a beauteous creature,' said the President.

'Thank you Mr President. You're a fair man yourself if I may be so bold sir.'

'You may my girl. You may . . . Now take it in your fair hands . . Fondle it and put it where it belongs.'

'There sir. There. It's in! It's in me! It's lovely! Better than my father's used to be! Fill me! Fill me! Oh! Ah! Come! Come! Daddy! Daddy!' she screeched over and over again.

Robespierre got up as soon as the President returned. He walked behind the trees while the President sat against another tree and lit a cigarette.

There was absolute silence all the time that Robespierre was away. About ten minutes later he emerged smiling.

'Today, sir, is the 27th of July. There's little time left. My Revolutionary Tribunal has failed me. Monsieur Saint-Just and I are to die tomorrow, sir.'

'My dear fellow. We are clement. Have no fear.'

'Clemency does not work,' answered Robespierre. 'It is our duty to the people to rid the land of counter-revolutionaries. The people first, Mr President. Their happiness, education, and the right to be looked after if they're weak.'

'Yes. Yes. Of course,' said the President impatiently.

'All land confiscated from suspects must be redistributed to the poor. The Revolutionary Tribunal would get them and the Committee would give out their lands.'

'Good! Excellent!' shouted the President. 'Exactly what I did after the revolution of July.'

'July sir? July? Are you French?'

'Yes sir, July. July sir. The twenty-third.'

'The fourteenth sir!'

'The twenty-third sir!'

'Fourteenth!'

'Twenty-third!'

'Fourteenth!'

'Twenty-third!'

Suddenly the President got up and went behind the trees again. He let out a gasp and returned white-faced.

'She is dead! Her neck has been broken. She is dead . . .' He looked around and could not see Robespierre. He called out his name. He received nothing but silence. He started to search for him but could not find him anywhere. He went back to Alia lying naked on her clothes. He held her head in his arms and started to cry.

'Oh mon enfant. Why does this have to happen to us? Why? We were so happy? Yes more of a question really,' he placed her head back on the ground. 'Happy? Fuck this dirty and miserable little country. I've always told my people that the Lebanese could not be trusted. We shall return to Egypt and work for our people. We shall do our best to destroy the enemy.'

In the morning the President walked towards the city centre to carry out his plans. His agents would be waiting for his instructions. He had to get to them very quickly.

As he emerged on to the airport road he found a group of people leading a prisoner with a rope tied around his neck. His eyes were blindfolded. The group was walking noisily with its members seeming to argue with each other and with nobody in particular. They arrived at the edge of the pine forest and sat their prisoner down.

Several of them went into the forest while the others stood around waiting. The President suddenly recognised the prisoner as Robespierre. He came nearer the group.

'What is going on my good man?' he asked.

One of the group burst out laughing and shouted to the others who had raised their guns, 'Don't worry. He's harmless. Let me present to you President Nasser.' Then he added in a whisper, 'He has been roaming this area since they released the loony bin lot.' The others laughed and raised their guns in a mock presidential salute.

The President responded by raising his arm to his chest and standing to attention.

'What is happening my good man?' he asked again.

'Well Mr President, it's like this. This motherfucker has told us that he has killed a girl in the forest. We're waiting to see if it's true.'

'I believe it to be true my good man.'

'Thank you Mr President. We will have this confirmed as soon as our men get back.'

'Of course, you need hard evidence. Yes of course. Well done. Carry on men.'

A few minutes later the group returned.

'Yes there's a dead woman in there. She's been sexually assaulted,' said one of them. 'We left two boys with her till they can come to pick her up.'

'Right! You know what to do!'

Robespierre was taken and led into the forest. Several other men followed.

'Where is he being taken, my good man?' asked the President.

'To be hanged,' answered someone.

'But you must not hang him. He must be excused,' shouted the President.

'Why should he Mr President?' said the man laughing. 'He killed a woman.'

'But he is mad. Let him go. He is mad . . .' screamed the President and ran into the trees.

The others followed him. As they got to a little clearing in the forest, they saw Robespierre hanging. His body was being lifted as two men pulled the rope. Robespierre's legs kicked frantically. One of the men jumped up and pulled his weight against the dangling legs. Robespierre's neck clicked as a line of spittle hung down from his mouth. It twirled and glistened in the sun. The President fell to the floor crying. 'But he is mad. He is mad,' he kept shouting as the tears rolled down his face.

'What's wrong with him?' asked one of the executioners.

'He claims that our rapist and murderer was mad. The poor fellow's really dotty.'

The gunmen walked away from the President in silence. As they passed him one of them threw him a five pound note and some cigarettes.

'Come on Mr President. Go get something to eat.'

'But he was mad,' the President choked.

'Yes of course he was, my friend. Otherwise how could he have done what he did? Go. Go get something to eat.'

* * *

Pierre disappeared for days. He walked around the streets of Beirut like a madman. His lust for revenge was overwhelming. He went into the deserted city centre and started fires in any office block still unburnt. Every time he started a fire he sat in front of the building watching it burn and laughing while talking to himself.

As he walked the city centre he kept talking to Marie's soul with a strong belief that it still hovered above him awaiting vengeance.

'As God is my witness. As God is my witness. Marie, your soul will be avenged. You will yet go to heaven my love. The motherfuckers will pay for what they did to you. As God is my witness.'

The very few who met him treated him as a harmless madman on the run. No one was interested in approaching this angy man who kept talking to himself.

Meanwhile Paul and Tamra were out searching for him. It was not too difficult to find him with all the informers available for money.

Eventually one of Paul's men spotted him and trailed him to Allenby Street where he busied himself setting fire to a clothing shop at the corner. Paul was contacted and arrived as Pierre sat on the other side of the road laughing and raving.

'Pierre.'

'As God is my witness.'

'Yes Pierre, yes. I understand. Come home with me. Tamra is waiting for you.'

'Tamra?'

'Yes my friend. Tamra. Your daughter. She needs you. She wants you home.'

'As God is my witness!' shrieked Pierre as he fell into

Paul's arms sobbing.

Paul took him to Jounieh where he would be in safe hands and well looked after by his own people. It was passed around that Pierre was suffering from battle fatigue and just needed looking after for a short while.

Soon Tamra joined them and spent a week with her father. At the end of the week Pierre had sunk into a morose silence that felt more threatening than his ravings had done. Tamra was exhausted. Her desire to get out returned and she decided that, come what may, she was going to go away for a holiday.

When Paul came that evening to visit them she told him of her plans.

'Where will you go?'

'Switzerland. I've got a chance of a temporary post in Geneva. I'd like to see the place and chat to the people offering the work.'

'What work?' Paul was shaken by the news and felt frightened at the prospect of losing her.

'Oh it's nothing definite. It's only a possibility. There's a vacancy at the U.N. working in statistics. I don't know . . . Oh Paul! I just want to get out for a while. I must get out for a while!'

'I'll come with you. I'd like to come with you. Do you mind?'

She threw her arms around his neck and hugged him to her.

'Well,' he said taking hold of her hands. 'Do you?'

'Do I what?'

'Do you mind me coming?'

'You mean you don't know the answer? You men are so ridiculously insecure. Do I have to spell it out for you?' She laughed for the first time in weeks.

* * *

Paul and Tamra spent ten days in Switzerland. They were like two teenagers in love for the first time. Tamra did not have to worry about anything or anybody. Her father was being looked after by Paul's relations. Beirut was a million miles away. She tried not to think of it and when news items on television reminded her of her homeland she switched the set off.

The two spent their days walking the streets of Geneva and taking trips on the lake. Tamra could not get over the fact that she could walk the streets in safety. Without fear and without worry. The trees were green and the houses were whole. The Swiss people were inordinately polite and always smiled at her and Paul wherever they went. The country was fresh and pleasant. And Tamra wondered if Lebanon would ever become like that.

'Yes,' Paul answered her. 'I think that one day Lebanon will be like this: peaceful and neutral.'

'At what price?'

'Switzerland also paid a price you know. Less than two hundred years ago Geneva was under threat of annexation by France. The Swiss civil war had its terrors too.'

'It doesn't feel possible today,' laughed Tamra. 'You get the impression that the Swiss shook hands before slaughtering each other!!'

'You know, they had their factions, local leaders, foreign interference: just like us.'

'Who was Mr Jumblatt?'

'Monsieur Frederic-Cesar de Laharpe.'

'Great name. Very appropriate. Laharpe. Arabic for war. And Gemayel?'

'Pierre Ochs.'

'Sounds painful!!'

'At least we only have Syria and Israel to contend with. They had France, Austria, Prussia, Russia, England and God knows what.'

'They're at peace now though. In our lifetime,' sighed Tamra.

'Not in our father's lifetime. Over seventy were killed or injured in riots in 1932.'

Even then, Tamra thought, years ago the Swiss had had their wars. They had had their atrocities. They seemed to have worked through them and to have learnt how to live in friendship and without war. Yet they, too, were multicultural and multiracial. Tamra felt a mixture of joy and envy at their deep-rooted peace and tranquility. Nothing could disturb that.

On their arrival in Geneva Paul had surprised Tamra by having booked two separate rooms. She had been worried about this but never dared mention it. It was as if he had understood her feelings and had done the right thing to please her.

At no point did Paul go back to trying to make love to her. He did not mention marriage as he used to before. He was extremely gentle with her and did nothing but show her concern. She had not felt so happy since before the war two years ago.

One of their trips was spent in an afternoon at Chillon. Both of them felt it very difficult to identify with Bonnivard. Lebanon's agony seemed to make his imprisonment a sojourn. Even then Paul noticed that Tamra was quiet in the castle.

'What is it?' he asked when they were on the boat again.

'Nothing important.'

'It was depressing. But somehow it doesn't matter beside poor Beirut.'

'I wasn't thinking about that. The castle reminded me of my mother. She used to read me a Byron poem. I didn't like it much. Even when Bonnivard's youngest brother dies I feel nothing. At one point the prisoner manages to see the lake after hearing a bird sing. A little window like our holiday here . . .'

'What upset you about it?'

'When he was released he felt – sensed – a regret.' Tamra made an effort to remember her mother's voice.

'Yet, stranger to tell! In quiet we had learn'd to dwell; my very chains and I grew friends, so much a long communion tends to make us what we are: even I regain'd my freedom with a sigh.'

'I understand,' whispered Paul.

'Do you? We've been at it for so long; will we feel lost without our little war? When peace comes will we know how to live?'

Paul did not answer. He took Tamra's hand and sat beside her gazing at the retreating castle, peaceful and yet once so full of agony.

She left Paul for one day and visited the U.N. buildings. In the late afternoon they met in a small cafe by the lakeside.

'How was it?' asked Paul nervously.

'All right, I suppose. But I really can't see myself being cooped up in an office counting meaningless statistics. It would drive me mad.'

'Thank God for that!'

'Why?'

'I honestly couldn't see what my life would be like in Beirut without you,' answered Paul thinking how easy it was to make such admissions of weakness in a peaceful and tranquil country.

'But you wouldn't have had to live without me, darling. You wouldn't be without me. We could've come here together. We both like it here.'

There was a silence which Paul did not want to interrupt for fear of hurting Tamra.

'Wouldn't you darling?' she asked again.

'No Tamra,' he looked away from her. 'No. You know that I'm needed in Beirut. I would never leave. I like it here. But this is only a holiday. A change. If I like it here that much then I must go back to my homeland and help to make it like this place. I'm not going to run away.'

'But if you got a job here then you would expect me to come with you. Worse than that you expect me to be in

Beirut with you even if it is worse than Hell itself.'

'That's different,' said Paul feeling very uncomfortable.

'Why is it different? Why is it always different when it is you men who want things your way?'

'It's different Tamra . . . I don't . . .' But Paul did not have time to finish. Tamra had got up and left the cafe.

He rejoined her at the hotel, but they did not speak about the matter again. They were due back in Beirut in two days and they were going to enjoy every minute before their return. Paul was adamant that Tamra was going to enjoy herself to the maximum. He was not going to upset her with speculative arguments about her rights or his rights.

It was not as if they were ever going to get married anyhow.

EIGHT

Beirut's peace was uneasy. People feared to walk the streets. Kidnappings, muggings, thefts, burglaries, and murder increased. Consequently, the prevalent pax Syriana was only comparative. There were no more wholesale massacres like Karantina, Tal Zaatar, or Damour.

Freelance cowboys took over the streets of Beirut and killed for fun or profit. Death by ideology ceased to exist. Death for the sake of the cause never existed in a country where fighting stopped on the last day of every month to allow the fighters to draw out their salaries and pay their wives their housekeeping money.

The Green Line remained ominously silent. West Beirut and its Eastern counterpart might as well have been a thousand miles apart. Very few people dared cross from one to the other. The courageous who did were of two kinds: streetwise businessmen and lunatics. By and large Beirut protected its money-makers and generally ignored the lunatics. There were a few halcyon days when people could cross from one sector of the city to the other. It became a kind of novelty.

The President had established his headquarters in a half demolished office block near the port area. This area had remained a no go area mainly because of the snipers who plied their trade of shooting like children having fun at a gallery on an English seaside resort. But the President and several of his ilk were never harmed. They were known by everyone and their madness protected them. Why should anyone want to shoot a madman? A harmless madman who did not know any better?

The President was one famous madman spared the bullet. Another such fortunate character was the Bibleman. The Bibleman would walk around holding his Bible over his head and shaking it at passers-by whoever they might be. He had an uncanny ability of finding bodies left after a night of kidnappings and killings. He would stand over the bodies and pray until the rescue services came and collected the remains and some times gave him cigarettes.

He was last seen running up and down the Beirut River bridge. He would run out in the middle and try to stop the scanty traffic. Cars hooted and avoided him. He kept doing this most of the morning till a group of armed men came. They got out of their car and asked him what he wanted. He ran to the side of the bridge and hung over it shouting and pointing. The others joined him and were unimpressed. Below, in the dried up riverbed, lay several bodies in various stages of decay. The men were very jovial as they gave him some money and cigarettes and told him that he had done a good job. They drove off fed up with having wasted their morning. A few bodies were neither here nor there. At one point in the civil war, there lay so many bodies that the meagre river flow was interrupted for a while.

The Bibleman was never seen again. No one knew what had happened to him. He might have been killed; some said. Others had it that he had gone abroad. A few hopefuls wondered whether he had been taken back by his Father after the way men had treated him. But this time there was no hope; they said. The Father had despaired.

The President would spend most of his days walking the streets of the city centre. Now and then he would meet Paul on his walks around the hotel area. And it was mainly Paul who kept him in food and cigarettes. In exchange, the

President offered him endless advice and historical parallels on the struggles of nations.

During this comparatively quiet period, Beirut was inexorably and inevitably heading towards another explosion. Its people felt it everywhere. They did not believe in the real peace promised them. With time running out, they worked hard and played even harder.

Amidst this simulated hustle and bustle, people disappeared from the streets. Some were kidnapped for ransoms. Others were taken for fun and raped and killed. Some were driven around and released after they had been petrified half to death. It was all a massive joke. Part of Beirut's daily comic opera.

The impotent government tried to establish its authority purely on a symbolic level. Thieves were arrested and released. Parking tickets were issued and torn up. One murderer was hanged in the public park. His body was left hanging there for some two hours and the event shown on television.

The hanging took place at seven in the morning as Beirutis were getting ready to go to work. School buses passed by as the man, still in his pyjamas, was half dragged and half walked to the gallows. He did not put up too much of a fight. He simply kept repeating almost politely, 'But I don't want to. I really would rather not.' Equally politely; a soldier responded, 'And who told you you had any choice in the matter my friend?' The question was almost clinical. Almost conciliatory; a sort of 'come on my dear fellow. We have a job to do and a long day ahead. And we haven't even had breakfast. Come. Come. This doesn't even count as overtime. Be a good fellow and hang quietly. All this is too embarrassing!!' So the prisoner mounted the scaffold, turned to the few curious passers by and waved to them. A few seconds later his legs were kicking for several minutes before he died.

And Beirut was full of cruel, soul-saving jokes about it. 'How many did he kill?' asked someone. 'Two,' came the answer. 'Is that all? My God we'd have to hang half the population after all!!' 'At least he had his pyjamas on for the eternal sleep.'. A few still sensitive souls said nothing. Their eyes took on a fraction more size to accommodate the new shock of senseless death and inevitable cruelty.

One day Leyla received a telephone call and was surprised to hear Paul's voice. In recent times he had been less unfriendly towards her. He seemed to be somewhat mollified by his expriences of war. Even then there were times when he sounded, and looked, inordinately cruel.

'Hello Paul. I thought you were going out to Jounieh with Tamra today.'

'We were. But I can't now. Listen. I need your help.'

Leyla was taken aback by the abruptness and directness of his appeal. He was obviously desperate and had to get to the point. No time to play the lengthy Lebanese social niceties games.

'What can I do for you Paul?'

'One of my friends has been picked up. Apparently he was picked up in Hamra early this morning. That's all we know.'

'Have you heard from his kidnappers?'

'No. Not yet.'

'What's his name?'

'His real name is Elias Salhi although he goes by the name of Johnny. He's twenty-five. Tall with long auburn hair.'

'Listen. Wait in your office. I'll come back to you as soon as I can. I'll see what I can do.'

Leyla started to make telephone call after telphone call. From the Red Crescent, to various Palestinian factions, Moslem splinter groups, and the individual lunatic fringe. Eventually, she located Johnny in the hands of a small group of West Beiruti gunmen desperately trying to raise money for arms.

She called Paul and told him to meet her at the Green Line. She went to the local PLO commander who was renowned for his intricate knowledge of every little nook and cranny in West Beirut.

'This fellow, he's a friend of yours then?'

'Well, actually he's a friend of a friend . . .'

'What a strange little country Lebanon is. Do you know that if you drew a friendship tree, a kind of friends of friends flow chart; you'd find that the entire population knew each other . . . Yes,' he added quietly. 'That's what makes it such a tragedy of a civil war. We're all good friends . . . Okay. Let's go. We'll get this fellow for your friend's friend's friend. Or was there one friend too many there?'

He drove Leyla to Hamra Street. They were accompanied by several armed man. Hamra was a sorry shadow of its old self. The once prosperous and sophisticated resplendently lit street had turned into a massive, untidy street bazaar. Its greatest legacy was Lebanon's ability to re-emerge from strife and trouble to start again: on the dirty pavement if necessary.

That undaunted Lebanese spirit could be seen everywhere and on every smiling face. Prices were rocketing. Produce was scarce. Luxuries were smuggled or stolen. Amidst all this Beirut survived and lived on. A practice run for worse things to come. An innocent, childlike people incapable of running their own country but able to survive one armageddon after another.

They arrived at a small apartment block conspicuous only by the large unscathed car parked outside it. Such a large car was an indication of the importance of whoever lived there. It was not so much that they had such a car; but rather that no one had dared steal it from them.

The commander went into the building while everyone waited outside. His gunmen deployed themselves around the area in a well-disciplined and orderly way.

When he emerged later on, he was accompanied by a frightened young man. He helped him into his car where Leyla sat waiting. The young man started shaking as the commander gave the order to drive to the Green Line.

'You're going to be all right, Johnny,' said Leyla gently. 'You'll be fine. Paul is waiting to pick you up at the Green Line.'

The young man looked up at her. His bottom lip trembled. He held his head in his hands and started to sob.

The Palestinian commander raised his eyes and gave a loud tut.

'There! There! Come. Come. We're all friends here. One big happy family!' he said cheerfully and tapped the young man on his shaking shoulder. There was not the slightest trace of irony in his voice.

* * *

Rashid's imprisonment had lasted over a year in the new camp. He had settled into a tedious routine of doing very little. After morning call would come a small breakfast followed by the whole day spent either under canvas or in a confined open area. Other than these restrictions, the Israeli guards were not particularly worried what the prisoners got up to or how much they talked to each other. As long as they remained within their specified area and behaved themselves they were left alone. Each 'cell' had its own local leader who organised and ran its repetitive daily life.

Rashid found it almost impossible to survive without something to do at the beginning. Eventually, he returned to his old dreams of Tamra and to composing poetry. A new dream had been added to these: Canada. In it he saw salvation. A new life. A new beginning. He soon learnt to conduct conversations with his fellow prisoners while continuing to dream. His mind was able to respond and his eyes to reflect without much effort. But his real concentration was on other things. After a while he started getting long bouts of depression caused by a kind of dream fatigue. The dream portion of his brain had become so strong that he slept nights for it and sleepwalked days propelled by it. Dream fatigue drove him to serious thoughts of eternal sleep. Though how he could commit suicide in such cramped conditions without attracting attention became an interesting chess-like problem and was added on to his list of dream amusements.

He was saved by someone giving him a smuggled pocket edition of a moving and passionate Arabic play in verse. It was an old paperback copy with frayed edges and yellowed sheets. The price he had to pay for this was to recite parts of it whenever he was asked to. He had to read it in secret knowing full well that the guards would tear it to bits as soon as they realised that he had a book with him.

Its earthy quintessentially sandy atmosphere suited him well. The heroine's death and her beloved's final collapse at her graveside moved him to tears every time he read that last scene. Yet he always substituted himself for the hero and Tamra for the protagonist – all the more fitting since he knew the impossibility of a relationship with Tamra.

The rumour spread like wildfire. Every prisoner was asking anyone who cared to listen if it was true. Was it true that there was going to be an exchange of prisoners? There had been rumours not long ago that Israel had invaded southern Lebanon. They had lost a few soldiers. This was bound to lead to an exchange of prisoners. Was this it?

Rashid sank further into his dream world as he desperately tried to prepare himself for the worst: a longer period of captivity. He tried not to ride on the prevailing high that filled the camp. It was bound to lead to disappointment.

For weeks the rumours continued without confirmation either way. Several prisoners were getting restless. The atmosphere became explosive and the Israelis brought up reinforcements as they sensed trouble coming. On one occasion shots were fired over a few prisoners' heads. One man was hit superficially. But this was enough to make the atmosphere even more tense.

Early one morning the camp inhabitants were awakened several hours before their usual time. They were lined up outside their compounds and told to move up one step when their name was called out. Rashid's name was called out and he moved up.

The process took a very long time. Those whose names were not called out were ordered back inside. The others were marched outside the perimeter fence where several buses were lined up. Their names were read out again and again. Eventually they were herded onto the buses. They headed north.

Rashid sat impassively being eyed by the two guards at the front. He said nothing. Inside, his heart was racing. He was soon to be free. To see Leyla and Tamra. His family. After two years. Or was it more? He could no longer tell.

As the buses arrived on the Lebanese border they were met by several United Nations officials.

A solitary voice in the back of Rashid's bus started singing an old Palestinian song. A few more joined in. Soon the bus was shaking with the men's voices singing with all their might. The Israeli guards glared a while, shrugged their shoulders and exchanged cigarettes. Outside, a U.N. officer smiled and waved at the singing men.

Rashid smiled back as tears rolled down his cheek. He could not sing.

NINE

Tamra returned to Beirut and enrolled at the university to continue her postgraduate studies in Physics. This time there was no opposition from her father. Since Marie's death, Pierre had withdrawn into himself and spent most of his time working solidly for the Phalangists. Now and then he would withdraw further and sit in his front room morose and thoughtful. As such times Tamra left him alone. He usually emerged from this gloom with a 'as God is my witness' and returned to his hard work.

While Tamra worked on her M.Sc., she continued to meet Paul on a regular basis. Their relationship had turned into an old and close friendship. They did not discuss marriage. Paul remained slightly aloof from Tamra while still disapproving of her relationship with Leyla.

With Leyla working full-time at the Sabra and Chatila hospitals, there were few opportunities for meetings. Nonetheless, the two women tried to meet as frequently as possible at the university which represented the only seemingly neutral ground during the few years of uneasy peace in Beirut. And the peace was uneasy. There was no longer an out and out war between the factions. Times had changed. Lebanon had been torn apart with mini states looking after their own. The Maronites started to rebuild their territory and before long they had their own economic infrastructure in areas like Jounieh and East Beirut. The latter was fast overtaking West Beirut in terms of business and a veneer of sophistication.

One day Leyla arrived to meet her friend with an excited face and a gay step.

'It's a rare sight these days in Beirut,' laughed Tamra. 'What's the news?'

'You're not going to believe this. Rashid is coming home. The Israelis have made a deal on an exchange of prisoners. We're giving them one of theirs back and they're releasing – oh I don't know how many. Rashid is one of them.'

'Leyla, that's fantastic. I bet your parents are pleased. When is he coming home?'

'They didn't tell us. They're having the exchange sometime next week.'

Leyla looked so happy at the prospect of seeing her elder brother. There were times when she despaired of ever seeing him again. She was full of horror stories about Israeli treatment of Palestinian prisoners.

A week later Tamra was invited to Leyla's flat. Generally speaking it was never particularly difficult for a Maronite to travel fairly widely during a peaceful lull in the intermittent disorder. It was harder for a Moslem to cross over to East Beirut than the other way around.

Rashid was still a short dumpy fellow though his hair had receded further. His face showed little sign of what he had suffered in the Israeli camp. He looked cheerful and still defiant. There was a twinkle around his eyes that endeared him to those meeting him for the first time.

He shook hands with Tamra and treated her with slightly exaggerated deference. Little did she know of his long thoughts of her during his imprisonment. Despite the loneliness of his confinement, or rather because of it, he had retained his keen interest in poetry. Tamra was fascinated by his slightly classical use of language. It gave her the impression of conversing with someone out of a historical novel. This impression was strengthened by the musty, gritty, and sandswept surroundings of the camp where they lived.

It was not long before the three had formed a close friendship group. Rashid, being of a very similar temperament to Leyla, got on well with Tamra. They used to spend long hours in the Uncle Sam's chatting about poetry with Rashid breaking forth now and then in his essentially effeminate voice. His right hand would go up and move in time to the heavily metric poems that he so favoured. He even wrote out Tamra's little sonnet full of South Lebanon's night air.

One day, while waiting for Leyla to join them, Rashid handed Tamra the sonnet.

She read it silently.

'Rashid, that's sweet of you. I've never had anyone write a poem for me. It's lovely.'

'A little soppy,' he laughed, embarrassed, remembering how he thought that nobody would ever read it.

'Not really. That's the man in you talking. Poetry is never soppy. You write something because you feel it. Anything you feel must be essentially noble otherwise it would not relate to genuine feelings.'

'For a physicist you have a lot of poetry in you. Where does it come from?'

'Oh,' stammered Tamra. 'I've always been interested. That's all.'

'You know what you were saying about feelings is true. The feelings expressed in this sonnet are genuine.'

Tamra blushed slightly and looked at Rashid's round face.

'No Rashid, please don't. Don't go on. It will only lead to one of us being hurt.'

'I know. I know. But I must tell you. I must explain. I wrote this sonnet sitting on a rocky hill in the south a long, long time ago. Tamra, all through my imprisonment the thought of you kept me going. I kept seeing your face. I kept thinking of you. As long as I live I shall never forget that fateful night. Not because what happened in it led to endless solitude and agony. No. It was the night when I knew that I loved you. The night when I knew that life without you was not the same. My life, destroyed as it was about to become, was going to triumph. To triumph because of you. Of your face. Of your voice. You kept me alive . . .'

'Rashid, please don't . . .'

Rashid's face registered a mixture of disappointment and embarrassment. He had expected this rebuff but was still hoping that things would work out. He felt embarrassed because he had asked for what he knew to be impossible.

'Is it because of my people?' he asked quietly.

'Your people? Rashid!! This is not worthy of you. How could you think that of me? Of course not. It has nothing to do with your people as you put it. I like you. I like you very much. It's just that I don't feel the things you have written about here. That's all. Please Rashid, don't spoil our friendship.'

She took his hand in hers and looked into his face. He bent forward and kissed her hand. She withdrew it quickly and looked away. They sat in silence for some time.

When Leyla joined them she could sense that there was something wrong. She guessed what it was from the look on her brother's face. She felt intensely sorry for him yet thankful at the outcome. She was pragmatic enough to know that such a relationship would simply not work out in Beirut. It would only lead to heart-break and isolation.

The three went down on the beach where they spent a happy day. It felt funny to be near the spot where Tamra and Paul had been that fateful morning. As Tamra lay on the hot sand she tried to imagine what it would have been like had she said yes to Paul. She still could not imagine the reality. She knew that she was being fanciful. She knew that the reality might have been sordid as love did not seem to fit into Beirut's soiled soul.

Soon perhaps, she thought. Soon things might work out. The war was over and Beirut would be rebuilt and would return to its old destiny. Then love would have a place for her and Paul.

* * *

'This is it!!' shouted Pierre. 'This is it. Those bastards are about to get their comeuppance. This is the day that I've been waiting for!!'

Tamra listened to her father with a heavy heart. In the background they could hear jet fighters swooping down on Beirut followed by a distant rumble as they unloaded their bombs on the Western sector.

She did not feel like saying anything to him. She felt disgusted by his ecstasy at the foreign invasion of his country. Moslem or Christian; all Beirutis were Lebanese as far as she was concerned. Her community's connivance with the invasion made her feel strong shame and fear. She knew that the tide would turn. Just as Syria was welcomed and then hated; so would Israel be. Lebanon, once again, was becoming a blood bath for other people's wars.

Her father left the apartment after changing into his uniform. Recently, he had started to grow a beard which made him look older and somewhat more sinister. Tamra listened to the World Service with intense fear in her heart. The news of destruction descending without mercy on every community filled her with awe. She felt a sense of admiration for people who could unleash such destruction and invincible power. Only the Christian community was being spared.

She heard of the atrocities that had been committed in the south. Tyre was in ruins. Sidon's entire population had been herded on the beaches. Masked Lebanese identified Israel's enemies and many just identified their own enemies and settled old scores. Israel's army was being dragged into the Lebanese quagmire of revenge and age-old hate.

As the siege tightened around West Beirut the fears in Tamra were replaced by a sense of defiance. She realised for the first time that the whole thing was a bizarre farce. Her people were standing aside like naughty children who had escaped their parents' wrath while their brothers and sisters were getting a thorough drubbing.

'Paul, this is awful. It's terrifying. Our people are being killed while we do nothing!! Why? Why?'

'There's not much we can do and you know it,' he answered irritably. Since the invasion started, Paul's irritability increased in the same proportion that Pierre's ecstasy had increased.

Whenever possible Tamra and Leyla spoke on the telephone. Their old friendly chats were replaced by strange and enigmatic statements. They spoke, intensely feeling their peoples' hatred for each other. Leyla seemed to have no bitterness. Just a survival instinct. Almost nightly, one of them phoned the other to talk about what was happening. At times the conversation would deteriorate into almost sick humour.

'I've got great news, Tamra,' Leyla said one night.

'What is it?'

'You know those pieces of furniture my father is always on about? How he left them in lorries when the Jews took over in '48. Well, they've just arrived!!'

They laughed unashamedly.

'How's life?' asked Tamra on another occasion.

'That's not the sort of question you ask in West Beirut,' laughed Leyla.

It was not all laughter though. There were night calls that had bitter tears and loud weeping. As a nurse, Leyla faced all the horrors of the casualties. And there were nights when she found it hard to cope, especially with the children. She would tell Tamra about her day and cry. At these times Tamra would murmur inanities without really knowing what to say.

Leyla did not feel that Tamra carried any guilt for her being safe in East Beirut while the West suffered so. It was Tamra who carried the burden of guilt. Leyla told her many times that she had nothing to be guilty about.

One night she went on the roof of her building and looked over parts of East Beirut and the Western sector. East Beirut was resplendent with brillians lights that zigzagged through its streets. Little twinkling lights winked at West Beirut in mock affection. In the West all was darkness. The only lights that Tamra could see were flashes of explosions the rumble of which reached her a few seconds later. She saw West Beirut as a massive rat-infested domain To the Easterners it did not matter much what happened there. They could hear it. They could see it. But it was away from them and they went on with their daily business.

Tamra wondered what anyone on a West Beirut rooftop might be thinking as they looked towards the East. What were their hearts full of? Would they ever forget this suffering and this indignity? There were people in West Beirut who might be foolhardy enough to have gone on the roof in the old days. Then everyone went up to ogle at others' miseries and sufferings. In this new war there was no distinction in the West. Everyone went into shelters. Nobody wanted to watch this particular show.

One night Paul invited Tamra out to dinner. She refused to go and he came around to see her.

'Why don't you come out?'

'Oh for God's sake Paul; do you really want me to go and stuff my face in some suave restaurant while people of my own flesh and blood have nothing to eat but fire? I suppose we could go to a rooftop restaurant and eat while watching the fireworks down the road!!'

Paul found it hard to answer this outburst. Although he did not feel as strongly anti-Israeli as she did; he felt a great unease at what was happening to his country.

'It's gone mad, Tamra. It is hard to know what is going on anymore. Some of us might be thinking that we are building a new Lebanon. But this is a Lebanon I feel that I don't want any part of. It's a Lebanon being built on hatred and betrayal. We are trusting an ally who's an enemy worse than any we will ever have again. Out of all this our only hope is Beshir. He would not be bulldozed by these murderers.'

'Murderers?' shouted Tamra angrily. 'You eat with them every night. You talk with them. You ask their permission every time you want to fart!!'

Paul flushed angrily and started to say something. Then he stopped, shrugged his shoulders, and walked away. He left Tamra sitting on a ledge staring out over the West.

TEN

Omar found it easy to get used to the noise of bombing. He knew that he would survive the day to day business of keeping life within him and his family. What he found hard to adapt to was the unexpectedness of it all. The Israelis seemed to have no rhyme or reason to their bombing of West Beirut. Explosions of all kinds were falling everywhere. Rumour had it that bombing raids were following information on the whereabouts of Yasser Arafat; the PLO Chairman. This meant, not only the presence of traitors willing to supply such information, but also that raids could literally take place in the unlikeliest areas since Chairman Arafat was not exactly blaring his daily itinerary over a loudspeaker. Every time local inhabitants heard rumours of an impending visit by Arafat their response was immediate and all-embracing: it's okay boss. Cut the goodwill visit. Can't stand the fireworks that come after it.

Nonetheless, these considerations were irrelevant to Omar whose main business was survival. In his little street lived several families who, like him, were not willing to up and go. The few that tried were turned back by the Phalangists and the Israelis at the Green Line separating West from East Beirut.

Omar called a meeting of the self-styled residents' committee. Several families met in the cellar of his building.

'How long is this business likely to last?' asked Samira, a corpulent woman who shared a penthouse flat with four children and the memories of a loving husband who had died of a heart attack.

'It's difficult to tell,' explained Omar. 'But we have to behave as if this is going to go on for a long time.'

Another tenant nodded his head solemnly saying, 'The Palestinians are calling it their Stalingrad. It could go on for years!'

'I doubt it!' said a young man sitting against the wall with a look of supreme contempt on his face. The others turned around and looked at him.

'What do you mean?' asked Omar.

'Exactly what I say. I doubt if this will last for a long time. We have not got the means to defend ourselves. We hardly have enough food and water. Our fuel has virtually run out. We'll be starved into surrender if not bombed into it. And since the Arab leaders are busy sunning their arses on the French Riviera; we're not likely to get much help. So, one can only have one conclusion: we won't last long.'

There was a lengthy silence as the group sat pondering what the young man had just said. A few felt shocked by his frankness. This was defeatist talk. Yet it was the truth. Nonetheless, Beirutis were not used to talk in terms of giving up so easily.

Omar was the first to speak.

'But whether we're going to last or not is beside the point. Salim is probably right although I hate to admit it, as much as you all do. We must think of our families and of how we are going to get through this.'

'Right!' said Ali who had referred to Stalingrad earlier on. 'Let's see what we need first and foremost. Salim quite rightly mentioned food, water, and fuel.'

'Medicines,' added Samira.

'Disinfectants,' shouted a person in the back of the small crowd.

'Toilet paper,' roared another and everyone burst out laughing.

Omar laughed along till everyone had stopped.

'We may laugh now; but he's right. We do need toilet paper if we are to avoid insanitary conditions.'

'God!' said a girl standing to the side of the crowd and smoking a cigarette. 'The more you think of it the worse it gets. Where would we flush all that shit?'

A few laughed. Someone suggested sending it all over to East Beirut.

'Good idea! Monsieur Sharon might like some to improve his image!!'

The laughter lasted only a few seconds. Omar allowed the small crowd to have its joke. He turned to the girl smoking a cigarette and smiled.

'It's a fair question Yasmin. With the lack of water it is a very serious question. We'll have to address ourselves to it as a priority.'

'At your convenience!' shouted Salim in English. Several burst out laughing and booing at the same time.

Omar continued. 'Now let's try to distribute responsibilities in a manageable way. Who wants to be in charge of fuel? We'll need a regular supply for cooking purposes and to run the generator.'

'What generator?' asked Ali.

'We have one down in the cellar. It was put there two years ago during the electricity cuts. It doesn't work as far as I know but we'll find someone who might be able to get it going for us.'

'I know someone who could fix it,' said Yasmin.

'Good! Get them to do it as soon as you can,' said Omar at the very moment when an explosion was heard near by. It was followed by several others. Shattering glass was heard as the small crowd looked at each other in the exasperation of knowing that they would be returning to flats that had no windows.

'Who wants to be a glazier?' asked Salim.

Several smiled wearily.

'There'll be a boom in the glass business when all this is over.'

Apart from speaking a little louder than usual, there seemed to be little evidence that the group were particularly bothered by the bombing going on outside.

'So back to business,' said Omar. 'Who wants to be in charge of fuel?'

'I do,' sang out Salim. 'Do you remember James Garner in The Great Escape? I'm going to be like him: I can get anything, anywhere, anytime! Just give me chocolate to exchange for fuel.'

'Good,' said Omar. 'How about food? Who wants to be in charge of that?'

'I will,' answered Yasmin, blushing slightly.

The cellar was temporarily filled with an air of scepticism as each person wondered whether she would be able to fulfil her part of the bargain.

Yasmin looked around blushing deeper.

'You have nothing to worry about. I know exactly where I can get the food from. Just leave it to me.' Her voice was so full of final authority that no one dared object to her assertion despite their doubts.

'Can I take charge of water? I did a course on Beirut's subsoil. Got an 'A' in it. I can magic water out of nowhere. There's no guarantee of its cleanliness. But it'll be water nonetheless,' a young student said sombrely.

'Excellent,' shouted Samira. 'You bring me the stuff and I'll cook it. I didn't do any courses in cookery; but I can produce a meal out of nothing. If you've had to cook for my children you'd be able to cook for all of Beirut!'

'There's one thing more that we need to discuss,' said Omar. 'We might organise ourselves too well. Others might decide to join us or to take over. We need to defend ourselves. We'll need arms.'

There was a silence as everyone in the cellar took in the implication of what he had just said. The idea of taking up arms against other Beirutis did not appeal to anyone. Yet they could all see that it might prove necessary.

'Do we have to?' asked Yasmin. 'Surely we can take in other people and help them without actually having to start shooting at each other. If people want to join us they would have to take part in the work too.'

'I agree with Yasmin,' stammered Ali embarrassed by too eager a response. He had been looking at her periodically since they had gathered together. She had noticed his looks and had tried to pretend that she could not see him. But now and then she looked at him when she thought that he could not see her.

'Let's vote on it,' ordered Omar. 'All those who agree with Yasmin put their hands up.'

Every hand in the cellar went up including Omar's. There was a general sigh of relief at the thought that they would not have to arm themselves against their fellow countrymen.

The meeting broke up as each person went off to work on their little area for the good of all. The air was full of innocent optimism that they were going to pull through whatever the Israelis chose to throw at them.

* * *

Rashid left the camp early in the morning with a small belt under his shirt containing a few dollars and a little notebook with his poems in it. He walked towards the National Museum area hoping to gain access into East Beirut and out. He had finally made up his mind that he was going to leave. He had said nothing to his parents.

The previous night had been a particularly bad one. The Israeli army was pouring all it had into the camp area hoping for an early surrender. Leyla had been working non-stop tending the wounded and the dying. She had no time to stop to think of what was going on around them. By late evening West Beirutis decided that the Israelis were deliberately attempting to hit key hospitals.

Late at night, Leyla had returned home for a short sleep before resuming her duties early in the morning. The bombing had subsided for a while. The Israeli air force was making sortie after sortie over Beirut and dropping huge flares to keep up the psychological pressure. Earlier in the day they had dropped leaflets advising the inhabitants of West Beirut to flee for their lives before the cataclysm hit their city. Most people laughed off the leaflets as childish attempts. A few decided to take the Israeli advice and get out through the routes indicated. Phalangist troops let a few Lebanese citizens through. Every Palestinian was turned back with threats and menaces against their life.

Rashid went into Leyla's bedroom and spent some time chatting to her. They had not talked like this for a long time. Sitting behind his sandbags for days; Rashid had composed a long poem called Lebanese Roulette. Leyla sat on her bed hugging her knees as he read extracts to her. His voice trembled as he spoke.

In Russia you had four chances
in five to live.
In Beirut you have one chance
in five to die. Now.
I need the Russo-Lebanese version.
If I went out of the camp.
If I spun the chamber.
If I cocked the hammer.
If I pulled the trigger (somebody
told me that it is the
trigger that pulls the finger).

Leyla covered her face and sighed. Her brother's mood had been apparent for some time. She felt her heart weighed down for him. He continued.

What if I felt a little scratch on
my temple?
What if I died?
What next?
If?

But what if I just hear a little
click and my temple intact.

Leyla uncovered her face and smiled. She held Rashid's hand and squeezed it.

What if?
The triumph of having courted
death and won.
I will play Lebanese Roulette
with
an
empty
gun – I like it better than
a
revolver.
Standing straight.

Rashid looked at his sister. His lip trembled as he read on.

'Am I standing straight, uncle?'
said the little Jewish boy to
his uniformed man who smiled
and patted him on the large head
and then shot him through it – once.
And they say that Himmler flinched with disgust as a bit of brain
soiled his uniform.
And forty years later
I refuse to stand still.
I have my dreams.
My verses.

Brother and sister hugged each other for a long time.

'Leyla, listen to me love. Whatever happens in the coming few days please only think the very best of us. We have always had a special relationship. Let us keep it like that. Just think of the good times. Don't believe what others tell you.'

'You don't need to say that Rashid. You have no worst for me. All in you is best. That and your poetry will always be what I'll remember.'

Rashid felt an awful sense of shame. Not shame at having to desert his people. His shame was for his inability to explain to his sister why he was leaving. He wanted to tell her. He wanted so much to tell her that he had received Arafat's blessings for his plans to leave.

Earlier in the day he had met the PLO leader himself in one of his many walkabouts in West Beirut. Rashid had been introduced to him and Arafat, who had an uncanny memory for people, had told him that he was honoured to meet a man who had suffered so much for his homeland. Rashid had asked to see him privately for a few minutes. Arafat had smiled and put an arm round his shoulders and motioned his bodyguards away. With a lump in his throat Rashid started to speak.

'I want to go to Canada,' he blurted out, regretting the speed with which he had said it.

Arafat had looked away in the distance for a while. He turned around again and looked at Rashid. His face was passive. It bore no regret or remorse. He touched Rashid on the shoulder and squeezed.

'Only you can decide that, my friend. You've given a lot to your people. If you want to go, then go. Good luck to you.'

Rashid was surprised by the leader's calm response. He did not quite know what to have expected. But in the recesses of his mind he had somehow half expected to be dragged off and shot as a coward.

Arafat looked at him as if he could read his mind.

'My boy. Palestine forces none of her sons or daughters. Go. With my blessings.'

Rashid started to cry and could find no words with which to respond. He had sorely needed the reassurance that no one would blame him for this. He had really had enough. He wanted peace. He wanted an ordinary life with a wife and children. He wanted to worry about his salary. He wanted to have nightmares about paying back a mortgage. He wanted to write poems. He so, so wanted a normal life.

When he looked up again, Arafat was walking away from him towards the small crowd that had gathered at a discreet distance from the two speakers. Someone whispered something to Arafat as several men whisked him away in a fast car. Within seconds, several Israeli fighters swooped down on the area and released their load. Rashid had hardly dived for cover before several explosions shook the whole neighbourhood. As he ran down several steps into a shelter, he heard the crash of rubble and glass just outside. The raid only lasted a few minutes.

As people emerged from the shelter, they were met with devastation beyond their wildest imaginings. An entire building had collapsed in on itself. No one knew how many were trapped inside it. Every able-bodied person started shifting stones and rubble in a desperate attempt to free the victims. Rashid joined the line of workers as they passed rubble one to the other. A few bodies were discovered and brought out. The bodies sagged in the middle and their heads fell backwards like slabs of fresh meat at a good butcher's. As survivors started to be brought out, the screaming and panic increased. Someone shouted that more Israeli fighters were on their way. The rescue teams stopped work and listened, looking up at the skies above Beirut. For a few seconds all was quiet. A tableau was formed. Several people were weighed down with rubble in their hands and a pair of rescuers stood with a bowed body between them.

The planes returned and swooped down a few times without doing anything. The rescuers continued their grim work ignoring the fighters. One man looked up at the sky and gestured with his fist. Several others laughed and shouted 'bang! bang!' pointing their fingers at the approaching fighters.

Rashid continued to work till late at night. By nightfall the rescuers had decided that they had got out everybody they could find in the remains.

Rashid looked around him as he wiped sweat off his face. Suddenly he felt tired. His arms ached. He looked at his aching hands and realised that he had torn the skin very badly lifting so many huge pieces of rubble.

Silence fell around the area as everyone started to go away. Rashid turned to start his walk back to the camp. As he did so he heard a moaning sound coming from a mound of rubble to his right. He started to walk towards it hoping to find another victim alive.

He climbed the small mound of rubble and lay down trying to listen carefully. He suddenly realised that the sound was not coming from underneath him but rather from in front of where he lay. He looked up.

A young man of about eighteen or nineteen was sitting on a square piece of rubble. His hand held his head and tugged at his hair at the same time. With his other hand he was picking up sandy rubble and then letting it go out of it in a soft, gentle stream.

Rashid could not quite make out what he was doing. He seemed to be picking up his sand from the side and then letting it drop in front of him on a small mound.

Rashid realised that the small mound was a heap of clothing, slightly charred and blackened. The man had obviously discovered the clothes of someone he loved dearly.

Rashid lay there looking and wondering whether he should go up to the man and talk to him. As he stared, the pile of clothes started to take shape. He realised that he was not looking at a pile of clothes only. There was a human form inside them. A small human form; also charred and disfigured. On its left, lay an immaculate toddler's arm which started to disappear as the moaning man threw sand on it and tugged at his hair.

Rashid turned around and slipped down the mound of rubble. He felt sick. He had seen enough death that day to last a lifetime. But that immaculate pudgy arm was too much. He reached the bottom of the heap and bent over retching and throwing up violently. He kept asking himself over and over again, 'Where is that toddler now? Where is he gone to? He was alive only this morning. Full of life. Utterly oblivious of this fucking war! Where is he now?'

All the feelings of guilt at wanting to leave Beirut disappeared. He made up his mind there and then that nothing in the world would stop him going.

After he had said his good bye to Leyla he had a short sleep. Early in the morning he started his trek into East Beirut. He was going to take advantage of the Israeli offer of freedom of exit. Surely they would want him to go. Surely they would not get in his way. After all, that meant one less fighter to worry about.

He arrived at the Green Line very early in the morning. To his surprise and unbelievable joy he was allowed to cross unhampered. He walked on down the main highway hoping to reach Jounieh and catch a boat for Cyprus. He was desperately dreaming of what life was going to be like from then onwards.

As he dreamt away with a light heart at his deliverance and a heavy heart at his hidden guilt, he was stopped by a group of armed men in a small car. They asked to see his papers. He showed them. They got back into their car and drove off. He walked on feeling that luck was on his side that day. A few minutes later he saw two armed men walking towards him. He did not pay them much attention. As they came nearer he realised that they looked slightly familiar. He carried on walking and ignoring them. A few seconds later they started to pass by him. He recognised them as two of the men who had just stopped him earlier on. He turned and smiled at them at the very second that one of them dug his gun into his neck.

'Get into the car quietly and nothing will happen to you,' said one of them. The car screeched to a halt beside them and its back door was opened. He was pushed in and they drove off at speed.

* * *

Salim drove gingerly amongst the spreading rubble in the narrow street. His car came to a halt near a small shop outside of which sat two men and a woman. There were several children playing around the rubble. The sun was searingly hot and the air humid.

'Good morning Salim!' shouted one of the men pointing to a small container of coffee. 'Come and join us.'

Salim smiled and sat down on a chair brought out by one of the children. He looked around for a short while and nodded.

'You've had a bad night of it haven't you?' he said.

'The best!' shouted the woman jovially. 'The best! Wished you were here.'

The others laughed and patted Salim on the shoulder.

'How many?' he asked pointing to the collapsed building at the top of the road.

'About forty killed and eighty injured,' answered one of the men in a matter of fact way.

'Night in the shelter?' asked Salim again to keep up the conversation.

'Cellar my arse!' said the woman looking around at the embarrassed men. 'I'm not gonna get dragged out of bed because of a few Israeli crackers!! What does it matter to me? What he does in bed is ten times louder,' she added pointing to her husband sitting beside her.

Everyone laughed. One of the children clapped his hands and ran to tell the others that mummy had just said something naughty.

'Don't listen to her,' said the husband. 'I don't do things like that! But I'll tell you what's really good about all this. When those buggers drop their bombs they make so much noise that for the first time since the kids were born we can scream out obscenities when we orgasm. Nobody can hear.'

His wife hit him playfully and ruffled his hair. The others laughed. The third man who had said little since Salim's arrival suddenly spoke quietly and with a misplaced serious air.

'You know something? When I was in England last year I watched a film about the Jews in Germany. And I cried!'

'Well what's wrong with that?' asked the woman with a slight irritation in her voice.

'I was just wondering if a film would ever be made of Beirut and its agony. And when it is, will any Jews cry?'

'Yes!' said Salim sharply. 'Of course they would!'

'Hey boys,' said the woman. 'Let's cut this philosophic crap and enjoy our coffee. It might be our last. The Israelis are planning a repeat performance tonight.' As she bent forward to pour out more coffee; Salim noticed a cross around her neck.

Salim turned to the woman's husband and asked to see his alone for a few minutes. They moved into the little shop where they sat in the cool shadow of the white walls.

'Have you got it set up?' asked Salim.

His friend smiled proudly and nodded.

'Now listen Salim. There is a convoy of food, fuel and medicines near the Green Line. The bastards are not going to let it through. They're letting nothing through. There was a policeman walking back from East Beirut with a sandwich. They stopped him and made him eat it before crossing over just in case he was taking it to anyone who was hungry in the West.'

'The bastards!!' snapped Salim knowing the futility of such an exclamation.

'What you have to do is just drive it across a few hundred yards and it's all yours,' said the man as if his plan were the simplest thing in the world.

Salim looked at him. He got up and walked around the shop a few times hitting the side of his leg over and over again as he desperately tried to think out a way of getting his hands on the lorries lined up near the Green Line.

'Let me think about it,' he said and left the shop.

* * *

'The fucking bastards are using phosphorus bombs. They're burning people! Burning them!!' Samira kept repeating as she busily prepared the evening meal for their neighbourhood group. Yasmin was the only other person in the cellar with her. She had been peeling potatoes and feeling very good at her ability to have procured this food so easily through sheer charm and nothing else. She paid very little for it. The farmer who had smuggled it into West Beirut kept calling her 'daughter' and loading her car with more. It was obvious that he wanted a little bit more than a father-daughter relationship with her. However, she responded as a daughter and kept calling him 'dad' which discomfited him completely. She felt that her response was a triumph. The poor sod's probably got a daughter her age at home, she kept thinking.

'Did you hear me?' asked Samira.

'Yes,' answered Yasmin irritably trying to smile. 'They're using phosphorus bombs. Bastards.'

'No. I said 'fucking bastards'! Ha ha so you weren't listening.' The two women laughed and tapped the table somewhat exaggeratedly.

'You know,' said Samira. 'We'll come out of this. We will actually win without firing a single shot. The Israelis will just get tired of Lebanon and get out like thousands before them did. We'll win.'

'And then we'll get back to normal again. Wouldn't that be lovely?'

'Yes my dear. Normal life. We can get back to the more intelligent business of killing each other. This is purely a family quarrel which we'll settle our own amicable way!'

They both laughed again.

Ali walked in looking unhappy. He sat and banged the table with his hand.

'Hey Ali, what's up?'

'Do you know what I've just seen?'

'What?' asked both women preparing themselves for yet more daily horror.

'They're using some new bomb that breaks up into bits and each bit explodes separately.'

'Is that all?' asked Samira disappointed. 'I thought that you were going to say that there is a shortage of such essentials as perfume, claret, and dinner table candles.'

Yasmin burst out laughing. A few seconds later even Ali smiled. Samira kept tapping the table and laughing as she pointed to his face.

'You Communists are so bloody serious. What's the point. What do you expect from the world? You're not gonna change it, are you? I bet you anything you want that when his wife took his piece in her mouth, Lenin dribbled and mumbled like every other male under the sun!!' As Samira laughed; Ali got up and left the room. Yasmin smiled blushing deeply.

Samira continued to laugh for a long while. She kept looking at Yasmin and bursting out laughing.

'Hey Yasmin, have you heard the latest . . .?'

'Oh no please spare me the sick jokes,' laughed Yasmin.

'I want to hear it. I love sick jokes,' sang Salim as he danced into the shelter with a broad smile on his face.

'What've you got to be so happy about?' asked Samira.

'Yasmin,' he said going down on his knees in front of her. 'Yasmin, you most beautiful of women. You are a true Jasmine. Will you marry me?'

Yasmin laughed and kicked him gently. He got up and acted out the part of the distressed lover. Samira tapped him on the head.

'I won't marry you. But I'll have it off with you if you want.'

'No I'm sorry Samira. But Yasmin is besotted by me. And that's all there is to it. She is dying to marry me. Aren't you dearest?'

'She might be dying to marry but it certainly is not you my boy,' shouted Samira. 'Virgins of the world unite you have nothing to lose but your hymens . . .'

'Stop it Samira. Please.' begged Yasmin.

'Oh I see . . .' said Salim. He walked over to Yasmin and put a gentle hand on her shoulder.

'I'm sorry. I didn't know.' He squeezed gently and walked away.

'I'll go and collect your little brats, Samira.'

'Wouldn't you like to add one to them my little fellow?'

'Not so much of the "little" please!'

* * *

Omar felt that Salim's idea was absolutely crazy. He had planned it too quickly and without much thought. That was the sort of man Salim was. An adventurer with a heart of gold. He would do anything, anywhere, anytime. Anything to enlarge his experience of the world.

But to think that he could steal several lorries' worth of food and supplies right from under the Israelis' noses! That was too much even for Salim. Nonetheless, there was an agreement amongst the group that they would not interfere with each other. Each person had his allotted task. Every other person would help in any way that they could. And Salim had asked Omar to get him a Phalangist officer's uniform and four or five Phalangist privates' uniforms.

Omar drove into the city centre in search of an old friend who would be the only person around who could procure such uniforms. He arrived into the hotel area and entered a small alleyway on foot. His car could never make it into the narrow road. He went well into the bottom of the deadend road and knocked on a large, badly-painted door. It was opened by a small girl with a frightened face. A woman's voice shouted from inside the house asking who it was.

'It's me, Omar.'

There was a quick movement behind the door and it opened wide. Before him stood an old woman with very white hair and a small pinched face. She smiled and put her arms out embracing Omar as if he were her long, lost son.

'Come on in! You are welcome. Come. Come in and sit down.'

The little girl followed them into the small room where they sat. Omar looked at her quizzically waiting for some explanation of her presence. The woman smiled at the little girl and held her arms out. The girl came up to her and was enveloped affectionately in a bearhug.

'This is Samia. She is staying with us now. She is a good girl, aren't you darling?'

Samia clutched on to the old woman and hid her head in her capacious bosom. Omar smiled.

'Our committee gave her to us. They found her in the Fakhani district after that last attack.'

Omar nodded and winked to say that he understood that the girl was an orphan. That she had seen too much. That she was slightly unhinged by her experiences.

'Listen Dalia. I need your help.'

'What can we do for you love?'

Omar looked at the little girl sitting in her arms and smiled again.

'Come on, Omar. She can't even speak! For goodness' sake we are not going to become like a bunch of Jewish committees in a ghetto suspicious of every little tilt of the head . . .'

'Sorry Dalia. Things have been difficult. We're trying to get some food and other supplies into West Beirut. We need some uniforms. Phalangist uniforms. These are the measurements and the ranks.' He handed her a piece of paper.

She looked at the paper and nodded her head.

'If you can wait till tonight and have a little meal with George and I; you can have your uniforms by midnight. What say you?'

'Dalia! If only you did not have that husband of yours; I would go on my knees and beg you to be my cherished wife!'

'Your cherished grandmother more like, you flattering monkey!'

The little girl looked up a moment and giggled at Dalia.

'God be merciful! This is the first time that she has giggled since we got her two weeks ago!'

* * *

Yasmin was sitting outside the shelter day-dreaming when she felt the presence of somebody behind her. She looked around and saw Ali sitting down on the step above hers. He smiled embarrassedly.

'Sorry about that,' he said.

'About what?'

'What Samira said just now about Lenin.'

Yasmin blushed again. 'Oh that's all right. I'm used to her talking like that. Anyhow she means no harm. She's only trying to cheer us up.'

'I felt a little annoyed with myself for walking out the way I did. I must seem such a fool walking out because someone said something obscene about Lenin!'

Yasmin did not answer. She looked out of the door at the top of the stairs and saw the sun streaming in humidly and harshly as it set.

'Would you like a coffee?' asked Ali.

'Yes please,' she answered regretting slightly the speed of her response.

'I've got some real stuff left upstairs. We can have a last clean cup together . . . I didn't mean it like that. I mean a last cup in the sense of for a long time not in the sense of our very last . . .'

Yasmin burst out laughing at his inability to get out of a slight mishap. He laughed with her.

'You look lovely when you laugh,' she found herself saying. The war, the bombing, and all attendant horrors had made her think that little politenesses were idiotic and out of place. If she felt like complimenting a man then why shouldn't she?

'Thank you,' he answered politely and awkwardly. 'This way.'

His small apartment was simply furnished. The front room had two armchairs and a sideboard with cups and other such implements for daily living. All four walls were covered with bookshelves with hundreds of books neatly stood in exquisitely straight columns. Through his window, at a dark distance over West Beirut, both could see the twinkling lights of the East. Lights that mocked the seemingly small flares, flashes, and fires in the West.

Through a small door was a minute kitchen immaculately kept with everything stored away in the most economical way possible. Through another door was obviously the bedroom and, presumably, the bathroom.

Ali busied himself making coffee while Yasmin looked at the lines of books. They were mainly novels, books of poetry and several histories. In a corner were a few works by Marx and Lenin.

Yasmin could not quite believe that they were both in a flat on the fourth floor of an apartment block; liable to be hit any second that the Israelis decided to mount an air raid. She just prayed that Mr Arafat would not honour their neighbourhood with a visit on one of his endless walkabouts. But up here it did not matter. The whole place was so peaceful. So out of this world. So poetic. Quiet. She loved it. And she suddenly understood why Ali was silent and reserved. This was his world. To him this war was an awful intrusion into blissful solitude.

'American coffee,' he sang as he carried a small tray into the room. 'My bottle of gas is almost empty. My last link with civilisation might be gone any minute.'

Yasmin smiled broadly at him as he sat down.

'What are you smiling at?'

'You. This is the most that I've heard you say in all the time that I've known you since you moved into the apartment – what? Five years ago?'

'Yes. I suppose that I don't say much, do I? I tend to live in a private world of my own in here. My books are my world. I enjoy nothing more than reading and writing on my own.'

Yasmin felt slightly embarrassed; as if she were an intruder into somebody else's very private life. She took the coffee that he offered her and looked into his eyes. They contained nothing but his inherent innocence and kindness. He smiled and she smiled back.

'What do you like reading most of all?' she asked.

'Poems!' came his reply fast and sharp. As if he were having a tooth extracted.

'Read me some.'

As if by some prearranged signal and a timetabling external to both of them; he got up and picked a book off the shelf.

'Come, walk with me;
There's only thee
To bless my spirit now;
We used to love on winter nights
To wander through the snow.
Can we not woo back old delights?'

'That's beautiful,' said Yasmin trying to control her tears. 'I didn't know that you spoke such good English. I learnt very little English at the Beirut Arab University. It's beautiful.' She felt slightly put out by the triteness of what she was saying. He felt embarrassed for her.

'I lived in England for several years. I'll read you another poem. A real favourite.'

He got up and picked a slim volume off the shelf. As he returned to his chair, a distant rumble could be heard. Several rumbles came nearer and nearer as explosions happened a few streets away from them.

Ali stood up and turned to go downstairs. Yasmin smiled awkwardly.

'Shall we go?' he asked.

'No. Read me more.'

He sat down and started to read his favourite poem amidst the shattering explosions, the sirens from racing ambulances, and the screams of the rescuers and civil defence workers.

'You do not do, you do not do
Any more, black shoe
In which I have lived like a foot
For thirty years, poor and white,
Barely daring to breath or achoo.

Daddy, I have had to kill you.
You died before I had time –
Marble-heavy, a bag full of God,
Ghastly statue with one grey toe
Big as a Frisco seal'

As Ali read; the explosions outside became louder and louder. Yasmin found herself counting the seconds in between the flash and the actual sound. And as she counted she kept pace with the metric rhythm of the poem. Some misguided Palestinian answered the attacking fighters with a burst of machine-gun fire that found an echo in Ali's

'Ich, ich, ich, ich,
I could hardly speak.'

The reading seemed to last much longer than it actually did. Ali's voice took on a staccato quality that sounded like someone else's.

'An engine, an engine
Chuffing me off like a Jew.
A Jew to Dachau, Auschwitz, Belsen.
I began to talk like a Jew.
I think I may well be a Jew.'

Ali stopped for a short time and looked out of his window. The sky was dark. This meant that they might get away with a peaceful night though they would probably get their usual psychological game of glaring flares and swooping planes. Yasmin listened to his reading without fully understanding what he was saying or what it exactly meant. It was not so much what he read as how he read it. His voice was full of a bitter hatred that found an echo in her frightened soul.

'Not God but a swastika
So black no sky could squeak through.
Every woman adores a fascist,
The boot in the face, the brute
Brute heart of a brute like you.'

A plane swooped very low over Beirut. It seemed to be coming for the very room where the two sat. The pilot, as he came down and in the split second before he shot up again after dropping his load, might have just seen the shadows sitting in the candlelit room. The city had just enough fires in it to allow him to see the two sitting: the man with a book in his hand and the girl sitting in front of him. To the pilot they must have looked like two lovers. Two lovers about to finish reading their love poems and go to bed to make long, and slow love.

A massive explosion took place very near the block of flats where the two sat. The whole room shook. The walls seemed to move as windows shattered and a door blew open. Yasmin fell forward and was caught by Ali who held her to himself for a while. As the shock subsided, he held her still and recited the last few lines without looking at the book on the floor beside him.

'There's a stake in your fat black heart
And the villagers never liked you.
They are dancing and stamping on you
They always knew it was you.
Daddy, daddy, you bastard, I'm through.'

Yasmin looked up at Ali's face. He smiled and let go of her.

'Stay,' he whispered. 'Let's not go downstairs. Stay.'

'I can't. Not now. I'm needed downstairs. We've got a job tonight.'

'Oh, I see.' He held her to him again and kissed her on the forehead. He kissed her again, this time on her lips. It was getting darker as fires burnt themselves out. He could not see the intense blushing that appeared on her face. She responded by pushing her body against his.

'I'll come up as soon as we get back,' she said.

'Yes darling,' he answered feeling intensely happy at being able to call her 'darling'.

'I hate this war,' she whispered breathlessly.

'It won't harm us.'

'It's evil. Everything's evil when it touches love.'

He held her face in his hands and tried to look at her through the dim light.

'It's so simple,' he said. 'If those evil men can get together to achieve their ends; why can't good men get together to stop them?'

'Who said that? Lenin?'

'No. Tolstoy.'

* * *

All was quiet on the Green Line. On the Western side there were a few Palestinian and Lebanese Moslem fighters who sat at a discreet distance behind several embankments of sandbags and mounds of red earth. On the Eastern side stood several tanks and armoured cars surrounded by many well armed and uniformed men.

At about midnight the Eastern observers noticed some movement on the Western sector. They started to look through infrared binoculars but saw little more than a few men walking away from their usual place of observation. In itself; this meant little. Nonetheless, the Phalangist guards decided to get in touch with their Israeli allies and find out what their next move should be. The Israelis boasted the best intelligence service in the world.

Almost on the stroke of midnight, five uniformed Phalangists walked up to the guards on the Eastern side. One of them was wearing an officer's uniform. He received a smart salute from all at the barricades.

Salim spoke with authority and a broad Lebanese accent indicating quite clearly that he came from the Byblos area.

Behind him stood Omar unable to open his mouth and hoping that he would not be asked any questions since his accent was distinctly Palestinian. The other three were Yasmin and two members of the tenants' committee.

'I don't like the movement going on over the other side boys. I want you to telephone headquarters and tell them what is happening. You, move those tanks over to that side. We're vulnerable on that wing. You there, bring me the keys to the lorries. You three,' he added, pointing to his own three. 'You get those armoured cars by the lorries over there. Now move it!'

Within seconds the place was full of the sound of starting engines and moving cars. As soon as the tanks started to move; heavy firing started on the other side. Shell after shell landed into the Phalangist columns. Both tanks were immediately disabled. The convoy of lorries started to move out at great speed. Five lorries went hurtling through the no man's land and into West Beirut. As soon as that happened firing stopped on the Western side. Omar drove in front towards the airport road and into the Sabra and Chatila camps.

As soon as the lorries were parked their drivers jumped out and several of the camp inhabitants came rushing out and started emptying the back. Omar and his group stood aside as all five lorries were emptied. A Palestinian officer came up to Omar and saluted smartly. Salim stood beside him smiling. He knew that the glory for arranging all this was his. But Omar was in charge.

'Your stuff is in that lorry at the end. Exactly as agreed. Nice doing business with you. Have a lovely day tomorrow,' he added laughing.

They all jumped into the lorry squashed happily together and drove into the city proper and into their neighbourhood. No sooner had they moved out of the camp than they heard intense bombardment going on. Somebody had taken the trouble of telephoning East Beirut and pinpointing the lorries for the Israeli bombers.

But Omar, Yasmin, Salim and their two friends were happy. In their lorry they had enough food, drink and fuel to last at least two weeks and possibly longer if used carefully.

* * *

Yasmin ran upstairs as soon as they got to their shelter. The others wanted her and Ali to join them for a little celebration after they had unloaded their lorry and disposed of it elsewhere. However, Samira whispered something to Omar who smiled and looked at Yasmin.

'Hey Yasmin! I think that you've done enough for tonight. Off you go. Oh and if you see Ali,' he added mischievously. 'Tell him that he's not needed. He can rest tonight!'

'Cause he's gonna need it!' sang Samira. Salim burst out laughing and ran at her.

'I'll take you up on your offer my darling.'

'Oh great. Hey Omar you couldn't unload that lorry on your own could you?'

As Yasmin ran upstairs she could hear the others laughing at Samira's crude jokes. She did not mind. She just wanted to be with Ali. And be with him now.

She knocked. He opened the door immediately as if he had been sitting just behind it for a very long time. He took her into his arms and kissed her hard. The kiss lasted for a long time. They went into the bedroom where they started to undress. He took her into his arms again and felt her nakedness against his. She pushed him towards the bed slowly. He lay down as she sat beside him on the edge of the bed with her hands on his chest. She stroked his chest and stomach. Her hand took his penis and stroked its hardness with a mixture of excitement and fear. She bent down and kissed it as she cupped it in both hands. Freeing one hand she stroked him between his legs and up to his penis as she took it in her mouth.

She remembered what Samira had said about Lenin's wife sucking his penis. She wanted to laugh because she felt so happy and so warm. As she sucked him voraciously and noisily.

The war had caused all her inhibitions to shed themselves and yet she was aware that she blushed as she did this to him.

Ali took her by the shoulders and pushed her down beside him. He got on top of her and she felt him urge himself into her young – very young body.

Soon the pain was gone.

He held her in his arms as they lay nodding off contentedly. They were woken by another crash as fighter after fighter passed overhead dropping flares over Beirut. Yasmin started to sit up by his side but he pulled her back.

'Stay. Stay darling. We don't need to hide. Our love will make everything perfectly all right. Everything. We shall live forever.'

He spoke solemnly just as he did during the committee's meeting. Yet Yasmin did not want to laugh anymore. She loved him beyond any love imaginable. Had she not just proved it?

'Take me again.'

* * *

Several people laughed as they saw the sight. Others came to their windows and stuck their heads out into the scorching sun. They too started to laugh.

Below walked Salim dragging, on a lead, a sheep with a bowler hat on. Two holes had been pierced for the hardly discernible ears. As people laughed; Salim waved majestically at them.

'Ladies and gentlemen,' he shouted at the top of his voice. 'This dear dear sheep, having had enough of the business of life, has decided to give all his worldly goods to your good selves. Therefore, you would be kind enough to present yourself if you would, tonight, at six at the main park outside known as the rubbish dump and we'll cook and eat this economic wizard!!'

The viewers clapped and shouted jovially. Soon the street was full of local inhabitants as Samira directed the operation for cooking the sheep. Meanwhile the meal stood to the side staring uncomprehendingly at all the commotion around him.

Very soon after he had his response as he lay panting and bleeding into the gutter with his eyes rolling around at the curious onlookers.

And by the next morning, he was a carcass on the rubbish dump.

Ali opened his eyes and found Yasmin sitting up at the bottom of the bed hugging her knees and staring at him. He smiled at her and she threw herself into his extended arms.

'Did you sleep all right?' she asked.

'I haven't slept like this for years.'

'Didn't you hear anything?'

'Nothing. Why?'

'We were bombed virtually non-stop all night,' she laughed as she snuggled up to him.

'Who cares?'

They got up and went downstairs. The others were listening to the World Service. Salim was interpreting the news for the others.

'It's all over. The Palestinians have agreed to get out. The U.S. has stood guarantor that Israel would not invade West Beirut.'

We've made it,' whispered Yasmin.

'Well I suppose it is a kind of victory,' commented Omar. 'But it's not over yet. Don't you believe those American liars. They would sell their own mothers down the bloody drain. You mark my words. It's not over.'

'Well boys? It can't get much worse can it?' said Samira. She turned to Yasmin and whispered to her, 'Was I right?'

'What do you mean?'

'Was I right about them dribbling and mumbling and whimpering when you got hold of it?'

Yasmin blushed and laughed.

'We're going to get married,' she announced to everyone. After a brief silence; Omar was the first to jump up and congratulate Ali and kiss Yasmin. Salim did the same.

'Ah! Yasmin you don't know what you've missed in not taking me,' he joked.

'I'm still available my boy,' sang out Samira.

* * *

The streets of Beirut rang out with the joyous sounds of people shouting, cars hooting and guns shooting into the air. The Palestinians were being given a noisy send off. As if to taunt their Israeli besiegers; West Beirutis came out in force to wish good bye to their friends.

Little vignettes of the Palestinians' drama and tragedy were being enacted everywhere. A man in uniform walked towards the pick up point carrying two suitcases like someone about to go on holiday. Elsewhere; a bearded man held his seven year old son at arms' length and looked affectionately into the face that he might not be seeing for a long time to come. The boy smiled back at his big daddy and looked proudly into his tired and shocked eyes. Women laughed and wept as they waved to the retreating army. A man held a woman who was crying to his chest. He covered his face and had his eyes shut tight in an effort not to cry in public.

An old woman with ragged clothes walked up and down on the side of the pavement holding up a piece of paper. On it, scribbled in semi-literate hand, were written the words, 'I'll take your place.'

Omar stood on the side of the road taking in the scene and cheering. His heart was heavy as he pondered the price paid for this retreat with honour. Beirut would never be the same again. His mind raced over the events of the last few weeks. He felt bitter at the way fellow Arabs allowed Beirut to take such a drubbing without lifting a finger to help. Never again would he see himself as an Arab – never!

Samira stood on her balcony looking down where she could see her children running up and down waving and playing happily. They had survived, she thought, which was more than could be said for hundreds of innocents in Beirut whose miniscule remains littered the graveyards and rotted beneath the rubble. Behind her, she could glimpse Salim asleep in her bed. She knew that it would not last. She did not delude herself but that he was a philanderer having a good time at her expense. It did not matter. She had not had a good lay since her husband had died. And Salim was good. She decided to keep hold of him as long as possible. Which she knew would not be too long.

A few floors below her flat sat Ali and Yasmin holding hands and listening to the noise from outside.

'What do you think darling?'

Yasmin looked into his solemn face and wondered how she ever fell in love with someone so serious about life. She touched his cheek and smiled. He smiled back.

'That's better. Don't be so damn serious love!'

For a split second he looked a little angry at her statement. He changed his mind and laughed, holding her to himself.

'I'd love to go with you to England,' she whispered. 'I can see us now sitting in a warm, little house in the middle of the winter with you studying with that serious look on your face. And when you finish your Ph.D. I'll go to your graduation and have a silly picture taken of the two of us with me holding on to your arm with a big tummy sticking out in front.'

He laughed at her dream. He laughed because he loved it despite its triteness and simplicity. He knew that it would be nothing like that. But still he loved it. Because he loved her.

And beneath them Beirut became quiet again. Beirut had undergone its change. It would never be the same again. Its scars seared its heart and left a mark for generations to come.

And amidst the joy of relief at being alive; Beirutis mourned. For their dead. For their injured. For their betrayal.

And most of all for those left behind.

ELEVEN

'Oh God, Tamra. They've got Rashid,' cried Leyla.

'Who's got Rashid?'

'I don't know. He disappeared last night near the Green Line. I don't know what he was doing there. We haven't seen him since then.'

'Leyla don't panic. I'll call you back.'

Tamra tried to call Paul at his new quarters in the hotel area. His people told her that he was out at his usual restaurant. She rushed there amidst the busy night streets of East Beirut. When she got to the restaurant she found him sitting with two Phalangists and three Israeli officers. She walked straight to his table.

Paul stood up and took her hand.

'I must see you,' she whispered.

'And how would our brother Paul like to introduce us to this charming and beautiful lady?' asked one of the Israeli officers.

'This is Miss Shami. Her father is Pierre.'

The Israeli officer was impressed by the well known name and shook hands with her. She hesitated in taking his hand until she caught Paul's eye. She sat between Paul and the officer who insisted that she should have a drink on him.

'No thank you.'

'But you must, my dear. I insist. Have some wine. Your local wine is excellent.'

'Is it?' asked Tamra angrily. 'You taking some duty free home with you?'

The officer burst out laughing and got up.

'We know when we're not wanted,' he smiled.

'Do you? Good. There's the road south!' shouted Tamra pointing.

The officer looked angrily at Paul. The three men said good night and left stiffly.

'What is it?' asked Paul trying to hide his anger and fear as they walked out of the restaurant.

'Paul I need your help. Rashid Salman has disappeared and Leyla's people are frantic. Could you help find him?'

Paul sighed and looked away from her. 'That's all I need now. You want me to go around negotiating for the release of a Palestinian fighter. For goodness' sake Tamra!!'

'Paul please. I know how you feel about all this. I know that you hate it as much as I do. You've had enough. But this has nothing to do with our feelings for the Palestinians. I'm asking you to help my friend. Our friend at one point. She helped you once before. You did it before in '76. Why not now?'

'For a start it was different then. Anyhow it was easier. We were in control. This show is not ours anymore. We've lost it to our great allies the Israelis.'

'Find him Paul. Please find him. Do it for me. Do it to show the Israelis that in the streets we still control our destiny.'

'But we don't.'

'I know. I'm only saying it because I'm desperate.'

Paul laughed and hugged her. She looked up at him as he bent his face over hers and kissed her.

'You've really got guts haven't you? Did you see that shit's face?' They both laughed. 'President Nasser would have been proud of you!'

'Nasser?'

'Mr Shah.'

'Do you see him?'

'Regularly. He comes in almost every day to lecture me and get his daily ration. Poor bastard!'

'I'm not so sure he's so poor. Paul? Can you do anything for Rashid?'

'I'll see what I can do. If the Israelis have him then forget it because they won't give him up. He will end up in one of their camps.'

'Camps?'

'Yes camps. The Jews had good teachers my dear. And one day the Palestinians will do the same. They're being taught too. We must thank Adolf for all this. Master race my arse!!'

'And mine too,' laughed Tamra, her eyes twinkling.

Later that night, Paul returned to tell her that he knew where Rashid was. A group of Phalangists, on very good terms with the Israelis, had him in one of their stockades. They would not let him go without a substantial payment. Leyla's parents could not afford a tenth of the sum demanded.

'Leyla, we've found him. They would let him go for a price.'

'Thank God he's all right,' said Leyla. 'How much do they want?'

'Ten thousand dollars,' answered Tamra knowing the futility of even thinking of such a sum.

'They might as well ask for the moon!' said Leyla bitterly. 'But don't worry we're trying to see what we can do here. I saw Abou Ammar today . . .'

'You saw Yasser Arafat?' asked Tamra in astonishment.

'Yes,' answered Leyla as if she were talking about the local tobacconist. 'He said that he would do all he could to get him back. He said that we needn't worry since he knew where Rashid might have disappeared to. He sounded enigmatic. I couldn't quite see what he meant. Oh Tamra, Rashid could not take another spell in an Israeli concentration camp. He really couldn't.' Leyla was crying and trying unsuccessfully to hide the fact. Her strength was ebbing slowly.

Tamra made up her mind to act to save Rashid. She would do what Leyla did. Go to the very top.

She left her father's apartment and drove around to Beshir Gemayel's headquarters. She parked her car at the bottom of the road and walked to the building. There were several men blocking the way with barbed wire, sandbags, and huge metal emplacements. One of them approached her.

'Papers!' he snapped.

Tamra produced her identity card. The man examined it and looked at her.

'What're you doing here?'

'I want to see Mr Gemayel.'

'You want to see who sister?'

'I want to see Mr Beshir Gemayel,' she said doggedly.

'Shall I also find out if his Holiness the Pope is available tonight dear?'

'You heard me,' she snapped. 'I want to see Mr Gemayel and I want to see him now. Go and do what you have to do.' She spoke with such authority that the man felt a little nervous. After all this may be the real thing. His officers would have his hide if he offended anyone of Gemayel's personal friends.

'Wait here please.'

He was gone for over fifteen minutes. One of the other men brought Tamra a cup of coffee and asked her to sit down near one of the emplacements. She did as she was told.

The first man reappeared looking absolutely amazed.

'Come this way please miss,' he said nervously. As they walked into the grounds he kept his eyes straight ahead and said, 'Listen sister. Please don't be offended by what I said about His Holiness the Pope. I was only joking. You know we have to be very careful. Gemayel's life is precious to us all. You understand.'

'Yes of course,' she answered feeling sorry for the man.

She was taken up a flight of stairs to a large, well furnished room. A man in uniform came in and asked her to sit down. He looked at her escort and ordered him to leave.

'I'm the Security Officer here, miss. Would you mind telling me what it is you want to see the leader about?'

Tamra knew she had gone too far. There was no getting out now.

'It's personal. I must see him personally,' she answered as loudly as she could. As she spoke she had an image of the woman whom she had seen hanged by the Phalangists for treason in the midseventies. She wondered if that woman, too, had a favour to ask. She felt frightened and tried not to show it.

'Personal? But you must understand that I can't allow anybody in just because they have a personal problem that they want to discuss with him. I'd have half of Lebanon in here.'

'Would you please tell him that Tamra Shami wishes to see him,' she said as imperiously as possible. Her courage was rising with her fear.

'Tamra? You're not Paul's Tamra?'

She was about to answer that she was nobody's Tamra but her own.

'Yes I am,' she faltered.

The man smiled and sat back in his chair. 'Why didn't you say so? Any friend of Paul's is welcome here. You wait here and I'll see what I can do.'

He returned in a very short time and ushered her into another room. This room was slightly smaller than the last one but exquisitely furnished. He asked her to take a seat and wait.

A few minutes later the door opened. She jumped up and looked at the man who came in.

Beshir Gemayel, the newly elected young President of Lebanon, was a handsome man with a shock of hair that made him look darker than he really was. He walked with a military gait as he approached Tamra, his hand held out.

He took her hand in his and smiled affably.

'I understand that you had been kept waiting. I'm sorry.

But things are very difficult these days. How's Paul? He hasn't been seen around here for some time. I hope that it is not you who are keeping him away from his duties.'

He spoke easily and with a smile on his face. He clearly did not expect his questions to be answered. This was just as well since Tamra was temporarily unable to speak. She had to shake herself free and try to look as relaxed as possible.

'I'm told that you're doing research at the AUB,' he continued, trying to put her at ease.

'I've finished for now. I got my M.Sc. last year.'

'In what?'

'Physics,' she answered wondering if she should call him 'sir' or 'Mr President'.

'Physics,' he smiled in mock astonishment. 'Our country will need women like you when all this is over. If this war has done little else it has taught us the value of our women to us.'

She remembered her conversation with Shah about building bridges. Although she knew that Gemayel's words were somewhat trite; they made her feel better. The man obviously had a strong charismatic attraction to everyone who met him.

'Well miss. What can we do for you?'

Tamra told him as quietly and as quickly as she could. He listened with a serious face.

'And you say this man is a Palestinian?'

'Yes sir.'

'And his sister is a very good friend of yours?'

'Yes sir,' Tamra answered feeling her fear rise a little.

'I see,' said Gemayel getting up and walking over to his desk. He picked up his phone and spoke to someone at the other end. His words were economical and sharp. He told whoever it was that he wanted Rashid Salman found and brought to his office immediately.

He returned to his seat beside Tamra.

'May I offer you a drink?' he asked politely. He was no longer smiling. Tamra could see that he disapproved. Yet he was acutally getting Rashid released for her.

'No thank you sir.'

The telephone rang. He answered it and listened a while. His face clouded over for a second. He thanked his speaker and hung up.

'Mr Salman is being brought here,' he said with a smile on his face.

'Thank you sir. Thank you. I will never forget this as long as I live.'

'No need to thank me. What else did you expect, my dear? I mean the man no harm. Now you listen to me carefully. We have a duty to our homeland to free it of all foreigners. I mean ALL without exception. Not only the Palestinians. I'm not handing this man over to the Israelis. I'm handing him to you. I want you to take him to Jounieh and to put him on the first available boat for Cyprus. My men will accompany you to facilitate matters.'

He rose to go.

Tamra stood up. 'Thank you again,' she said with intense relief.

'You're welcome miss,' he answered and left the room. An officer returned a few seconds after he had left. He asked Tamra to accompany him.

When they reached the entrance downstairs; there was a car waiting with armed men standing around it.

'Who is it?' asked one of the gunmen trying to look into the car.

'It's Yasser Arafat,' answered another. 'They're trying to get him out of Beirut.'

'You're not serious?'

'Shshshsh. Not so loud. This is top secret. They're trying to get him away from the Israelis.'

'Why?' whispered the first speaker. 'Let'em have him.'

'No. If they had him they would give him a fair trial and hang him. We want to pickle his balls and fry his prick for Christmas . . .'

Several men burst out laughing and started jokingly to hit the first speaker. They all stopped when they saw

Tamra and the officer. She was led to the car and ushered in. In the back seat sat Rashid. His face was bruised and he looked sick and tired. He looked at Tamra and tried to smile. The attempt obviously hurt. She told him to sit still and rest.

'Right miss,' said their driver. 'We're off to Jounieh. Lovely ride tonight.' He was a cheery old fellow who kept up a constant chatter all the way. Their car was accompanied by two jeeps full of armed men.

As the driver chatted happily Tamra took Rashid's hand in hers and squeezed it. They held hands all through the journey. In Jounieh the armed men walked them to the boat and stood beside them while they said their goodbyes. Both knew that they could not speak freely. It was very difficult not to have said a word to each other, not to have been able to ask Rashid what had happened to him.

'Bye Rashid,' said Tamra in as matter of fact way as possible. 'I'll call tonight and tell them you're all right.'

'Yes,' he spoke hoarsely. 'Do, love.'

'Give us a call from Cyprus.'

'I'll try. You know what the lines are like. I'll be going to Canada. I'll write eventually. Canada is beautiful, they say.'

'Yes. Poetic.'

Rashid smiled and walked away. One of the gunmen asked another if he was a Palestinian.

'No he's a man from Mars. Do you really think we'd let a Palestinian leave with his balls still dangling you little turd?'

'What about his accent then?'

'Southern Lebanese you thick idiot. Or maybe he's a Palestinian working for us. In which case they're allowed to retain their balls for entertainment.'

'And you're not likely to retain yours for long if you don't get this lady back to East Beirut this very second!!' shouted their officer.

* * *

Both Pierre and Paul were absolutely staggered by Tamra's audacity. Not only had she managed to get to see Beshir Gemayel; she had actually got him to have a Palestinian released. Paul said that that was the kind of thing that he had always expected from Gemayel. Pierre said that he was a fool to release him.

'Should've shot the fucking bastard's balls off,' he declared as he left the room.

Leyla received the news of her brother's release very calmly. She kept telling Tamra that she loved her.

'I wish we could meet Tamra. If we could only have one day together like we used to.'

'We will soon. It looks as if Habib is sorting this mess out.'

'Yes,' said Leyla. She had to be careful over the telephone. She wanted to tell Tamra that she did not believe in American promises. That she no longer trusted the Arabs. She trusted no one. She so wanted to talk like they used to do.

'Yes, of course,' she repeated.

'I understand Leyla,' said Tamra. 'I honestly do.'

'Must say good bye now. I'm on duty in ten minutes.'

'Bye. See you soon.'

'Yes, of course, love. Good bye. Say hello to Paul for me.'

'I will. Bye.'

* * *

Paul sounded breathless on the phone.

'What is it Paul? What has happened?'

'There's been a massive bomb in Beshir Gemayel's headquarters. The president is injured but all right thank God.'

'Come round love. I want to see you.'

'I can't. Not now. We've been placed on alert. I won't see you for a few days. I'm going home.'

She knew that he meant Jounieh. He could not say so over the telephone.

Her father returned home very late that night. They sat together chatting until the early hours of the morning.

It was such a long time since they had had some time together. Her father seemed at his most normal. He talked of Marie and the old days with gentle nostalgia.

'Do you remember when you were choosing your courses at university? Marie made my life hell over you doing Physics. She really was a dynamic woman. Well, she's had her way, thank God. You have done Physics.'

'You don't mind; do you daddy?' she asked talking as she used to before all this carnage started.

'Of course not. It seems such a stupid objection now. It doesn't make any difference now that we've been through all this. We're different.'

'Are we?'

'Yes. Things aren't the same anymore. They never will be.'

'They will dad. When all this is over, Lebanon will be as it always used to be.'

'But there are too many scars my love. We are so badly scarred we will never be able to get back to our old life.'

'We don't want to get back to our old life anymore. We want a new one. We want a new life where we would all be judged on merit and not on our religion. There will be a new Lebanon. There has to be. It just seems impossible now. Listen daddy, if we try to . . .'

She did not finish her sentence. There was a loud explosion near their apartment building. This was followed by continuous machine-gun fire that was so loud that it seemed to shake the whole neighbourhood. Pierre walked to the window and looked out.

'It's our people. They are shooting at everything. What's going on?'

He ran out of the apartment with Tamra running after him.

'Father, come back. Come back,' she shouted. By the time she reached the ground floor he had gone outside. Within seconds he was back again.

'What is it father?' she asked as she saw his face.

He looked at her for a while. His eyes started to well up with tears. He took her hand in his and said. 'The president is dead. Beshir is dead. They've killed him. As God is my witness!!!'

TWELVE

Dusk is descending on Beirut. The red sky reflects seemingly endless colours. The whole city lies peaceful and quiet. Its inhabitants have withdrawn for the night. Like the frightened, little harmless creatures that they have become they scurry into their bowers for safety. Nothing can get worse than it has been for the last few weeks. Life is returning to normal. President Gemayel's death has stunned the city into the silence of eternity. Beneath its red glowing sky, Beirut withdraws into itself to count the price it is about pay.

Out of the city's southern route comes a convoy of cars and jeeps. They move slowly and in an orderly fashion. Their destinations are the camps of Sabra and Chatila in the southern sectors of the city.

The camps have been closed off by the Israeli Army. No one is allowed to leave. A few hardy Israeli soldiers do not approve of what is happening. The camps are a ghetto.

'We might as well be in Poland or Russia,' says a young Israeli soldier to his friend. 'Look. We're closing the gates on them for the night.'

'We are protecting them.'

'Is that what you call it these days. I thought I heard my father call it a pogrom. Saturday night entertainment. Crystal night.'

'Never mind then. It's not Saturday tonight, is it? And there is little glass in there. So relax and do what you're told,' answers the friend jovially.

'I vas only obeying ze orders!!' snaps the young soldier nervously.

As they speak, a long line of cars starts to inch its way towards their checkpoint. The front car slows down near them.

'Are they all in there, friend?'

'Not one of them has been allowed out,' answers the Israeli soldier. 'Not one.'

'Good,' says the Lebanese driver. 'They're all safe then ... We're going in to look after them,' he laughs and smiles all around. His friends in the car join in his laughter.

The jovial Israeli soldier waves them on. 'Ma-islamah.'

'Shalom!' shout several of the car's occupants.

The cars are parked just outside the camp. Several men and women line up in front of their leader.

'You know what to do. I want a clean job. A tidy job.'

Several groups go different ways. Soon they are all swallowed up by the squalid alleys and by ways of the camps.

One such group is made up of seventeen men and two women. Their leader calls them together for a pre-battle chat.

'Now listen, brothers. Don't give the motherfuckers a chance. The place is crawling with Palestinian terrorists. Rid Lebanon of the bastards. Kill every single cunt you can get your hands on. Leave no one. Take no prisoners. Take no prisoners.'

'Take no prisoners,' the group chants. 'Take no prisoners. We're in your hands Pierre. We're behind you boss.'

Pierre takes in a deep breath. Since Marie's death he has been waiting for this opportunity to exact his revenge. The time has come to free Marie's tormented soul. To exact the price for her death.

Pierre strokes his bushy ginger beard, hugs his machine-gun, and walks down the alleyway. His group surround a small hovel of a house and kick the door down. Within, a family are at supper. The father jumps up and shouts, 'Don't shoot! For God's sake! The children!' Before he has even finished his sentence the room is filled with the crackling of firearms. He falls backwards on the table. His wife screams and holds the child closest to her. Within seconds the room is silent again. The floor is littered with the debris of the family's meal, furniture, and bodies.

'Well done everybody. Let's get more of the mother-fuckers,' shouts someone.

As they walk down the alley, a little boy of about seven appears. He is crying. One of the women goes forwards to him and says, 'What's the matter my little fellow?'

The boy looks at her and dares not answer. His bottom lip trembles as a shriek is heard behind him. A woman comes running forward screaming. 'Please. Ya Allah. Ya Allah. Leave my little boy alone.'

Behind her run two girls and a young man.

'Is this boy yours?' asks Pierre.

'Yes sir. Yes sir, he is. Please let us go.'

'Why should I let a whore like you go?' asks one of the women.

'Yes. Yes. That's what I am. A whore. You can have me. But let the little ones go. Do what you want with me. Just let them go. They're orphans.'

'Where's their father?' asks Pierre his heart hardening.

'Dead sir. He's dead. He died in Karantina. We've been alone since then.'

'You were from Karantina you fucking bitch,' says Pierre as he strikes her across the face with the butt of his machine-gun. The woman falls over and her children stand fixed to their places. The little boy runs forward and throws himself on his mother. 'Leave my mummy alone!' he screams.

'Stand up you filthy Palestinian cunt!' squeals someone. 'Stand up!' She does and puts her arms around her little son.

'It's your lucky day today,' says Pierre. 'I'm going to let you go on one condition.'

'Thank you sir. Thank you. Anything you want!' pleads the woman adjusting her scraf around her head as if she is about to be taken out on a Sunday outing.

'I'm going to let you go on one condition,' repeats Pierre. 'You can take your favourite child and I'm blowing the others to Hell. Make your choice sister.'

The woman lets out an animal shriek that shakes even some of Pierre's battle-hardened men and women.

'In the name of your God. In the name of Jesus Christ. In the name of all that's precious to you. Your children. Your poor mother. Your lovely wife . . .' As she says 'wife' Pierre hits her again and she falls backwards.

'You will all die. Now! If you don't choose, you mother of whores. Now!!' He fires a few rounds in the air.

The woman jumps up and clutches her seven year old. She is trembling and sobbing. She does not look at her other children. Her eldest boy lunges forwards and throws himself at one of the men. Before he can even move two steps he is felled. Pierre hits the woman and snatches her boy out of her arms.

'No! No! We are on your side. We're from Nazareth!' She screams over and over again. Pierre pulls the boy's hair back and with one swing of his arm he cuts his throat. The boy falls forward. His body shakes as he dies.

For a split second everyone stands staring at the quivering body. The mother makes deep guttural noises that sound like a cow having her throat cut.

'Fuck 'em and kill 'em!!' shouts Pierre to his men walking away from the scene. As he approaches the corner he hears a man sobbing. He lifts his gun and turns. One of his men is leaning against the wall being sick.

'What the fuck is wrong with you?' shouts Pierre above the screams of the three women.

'Nothing sir!' answers the man as he stands to attention.

'Don't like the sight of blood. You think it cruel, I

suppose. That little fucker would have grown up to rape your sister and your mother. Is that what you want? Do you want Lebanon to be dirtied by such fucking scum? Go to Damour and look what the scum did. Go!' He points southwards. Women are heard moaning and men shouting.

'They did what we did. They did what we're doing here. They'll do it after we've done it here ...' The man is shrieking at his officer in his young, angry voice. 'He was a bloody kid. A fucking little boy like my son at home. You actually took pleasure in doing it you bastard ...'

He does not get a chance to finish what he has to say. A hail of bullets hits him from behind Pierre. Pierre looks around and sees one of his women standing there.

She walks up to the dying man and points her machine-gun at him. She opens up and does not stop until she has run out of ammunition. The dead man's body shivers as tens of bullets tear through it.

'It's shits like him who lost us Gemayel,' she whispers and spits at the body. 'Not even man enough to want to fuck. Cries instead. Let's go sir. We've got a lot of work to do. If we don't finish it no one else will.'

They walk on amidst the men's laughter and the women's screams and moans.

* * *

Leyla first knew of the massacre while at the hospital where she worked. Patients started arriving as complete darkness covered the camp. The Israelis were firing flares to light up the camp at the request of the Phalangist troops. The carnage was continuing well into the night.

Leyla slipped out of the hospital and ran towards her home. She found her father and mother hiding in the little front room.

'You've got to get out of here. They're killing everybody. Come with me. You can hide in the hospital.'

'No,' said her father. 'You stay with your mother. I'm

going to get my son. He's at the clinic. We'll get out together.'

'I must get back to the hospital father,' she pleaded.

'Go love. Go. And may God be with you. I'll be all right alone for a while,' said her mother.

Leyla's father rushed out of the house and ran as fast as he could to the clinic where his son worked. From the gunfire behind him he estimated that it would take the troops about half an hour to get to his area. He found his son frantically helping wounded people into cars.

'Come son. Your mother needs us to get her out of here,' shouted the father above the hustle and bustle of stretcher bearers.

'I'm not going father,' the son answered without looking up. 'I'm needed here. I'm not going. You go. Please. Take the northern route. That might still be open. Go!'

The old man hesitated a while. He put his arms out and his son fell into them.

'Don't worry father. We'll be all right.'

'Not so long ago since I bounced you on my knees my boy. You have grown into a big man. . . Proud of you. Stay my boy. Stay where you are needed. . .' he added pointing to the tens of victims lying and half sitting on the dusty ground. Some were whimpering, others weeping. A few sat or lay motionless with a glazed look in their eyes. A couple of men stretched their arms out as if wanting something. When asked what they wanted they flopped back and sighed.

'Next year in Jerusalem, my boy. Right. Home!!'

'Yes father,' choked Imad.

The old man ran out and headed towards his home. He found his wife waiting for him at the door. She did not ask him where their son was. She knew that her boy would not go. Just as she knew that Leyla would stay.

As they reached the northern exit route from the camp they were met by a group of Palestinian women and children trying to get out. An Israeli soldier was pointing a gun and shouting at them to get back.

'You will be all right. Get back and stay in your homes,' she shouted.

Several voices clamoured for a way out.

'They're shooting everybody,' shouted someone.

'No they're not,' answered the soldier. 'Now get back. They are only mopping up the last pockets of resistance. You'll be safe as long as you stay at home and give up your weapons.'

'But we have no weapons,' screamed a woman. 'For God's sake let the children out. We'll stay. Just take the children out.'

A childish voice was heard shouting, 'I'm not going without you mummy.'

'Get back!!' The soldier fired a few shots above their heads. The crowd dispersed in all directions.

Leyla's parents found themselves in a small alley at the bottom of which stood two white horses. The horses were restless. They kicked at the walls behind them and champed at their bits.

'Look husband. Look. Even the dumb animals can't escape. What will happen to the children?'

'They'll be all right, mother. They are young. They are strong. They will survive.'

'I've got me two old'ens here boys,' shouted someone. Mr and Mrs Salman looked around and saw several men walking towards them guns at the ready.

'Two beauties. Magnificent stallions. Two humans are ugly specimens though,' said one and the others laughed.

The couple held each other tight.

'The children father?'

'They'll be all right mother. All right. In the name of Allah the Merciful the Compassionate. Take it easy mother. We're not going to show 'em fear, are we mother?' as he put his hand on her eyes. He looked at the men coming towards them.

'Jerusalem! Jerusalem!' he shrieked as the men opened fire.

* * *

Pierre's appetite is being further whetted by the sweet taste of revenge. Marie's soul hovers above encouraging him. He is convinced that he can hear her voice urging him to go on. For the first time in several years he is the victor. His is the way. Lebanon will be pure again. Its air will be his. Its mountains will reflect the white purity of his own aspirations. Lebanon will be fit for his Tamra to live in.

He continues his walk with his group. He encourages his men and women to hide traces of their deeds. Bulldozers are brought in in a clumsy attempt to cover up the bodies.

Early in the morning he sends a message to his Israeli contact telling him that he and his people have got rid of some three hundred terrorists.

The terrorists lie in alleyways, under rubble, in the streets resting against Eucalyptus trees and blood-stained walls.

* * *

Midday and the news came that the troops were nearing Leyla's hospital area. A frantic attempt was made to move the less seriously wounded. Cars and jeeps were requisitioned to ferry the injured to safer parts of the camp.

By the afternoon, only the most seriously wounded were left in the hospital. A huge red crescent flag was displayed from an upper story balcony. Some of the doctors and nurses accompanied the injured as they were being taken away.

'Go Leyla.' said an Egyptian doctor. 'You must go.'

'No. I'm not going. This is where I belong. This is my home. I have no where to go. No where.' She started to cry.

'I know love. I understand. But if you went you will be of use with the injured who need you most.'

'These people need me,' she said pointing at the serious cases lying on the hospital floor. 'They need me. I'll never leave them. This is a hospital. They won't bother us. Where are all those great promises from Reagan? Where have all Habib's promises gone? Why did the PLO believe them?'

'They wouldn't be the first promises broken by those people. Don't bother to explain it ...' said Doctor Ibrahim.

Leyla stood up straight. She wiped her eyes. 'I'm sorry. I'm making a fool of myself. I should've known better than to come out with such rubbish. Mr Reagan is on holiday recovering from the rigours of office!!' She smiled at her friend who smiled back at her.

'Come out with your hands over your heads and no harm will come to you or to your patients,' said a voice over a loudspeaker outside the hospital. The speaker had a southern Lebanese accent.

'Stay here Leyla. I'll go and talk to them.'

Leyla could see him walking towards the commander of the troops outside. He walked with his arms up in the air but with a certain incontestable dignity. A few words were exchanged but she could not hear anything. The commander seemed angry about something. He kept pointing to the hospital and then pointing towards the airport road. He obviously wanted everyone out.

Doctor Ibrahim returned a few minutes later.

'There's going to be an air raid. He wants all patients and staff removed immediately.'

'But we can't move those people,' protested Leyla.

'He is calling for ambulances and ambulance crews. They will do the moving.'

'Do you believe him?'

Doctor Ibrahim looked at Leyla with large, sad eyes.

'What choice do we have? If we resist we're dead. So are they. This way we might all have a chance.'

Leyla and the doctor called the six other nurses who had stayed behind. They were very frightened. One was sobbing and talking at the same time. 'Tell them we're Lebanese. We're Lebanese. We're not Palestinians!!'

'Shut up!!' snapped Ibrahim.

Leyla went up to the hysterical nurse and put an arm around her. 'Don't be frightened love. They won't hurt you. They're not looking for Lebanese health workers. They'll let us all go. Just take it easy.'

'You're the only Palestinian Leyla. Just you. Why the fuck don't you go?'

Leyla stepped back and looked at Ibrahim. The crying nurse also looked at him.

'I'm sorry,' she whispered.

'That's all right love. Let's go,' said Leyla.

They walked out of the hospital with their hands up. As they did so they saw to their left a fleet of ambulances coming towards them. Leyla's heart jumped for joy when she saw the Red Cross flags fluttering on either side of each ambulance. So they had meant it. They really were taking them all to safety.

The commander came forward and said quietly, 'Put your hands down everybody. Put your hands down. This is not a surrender. We're not fighting a war.' He smiled pleasantly at everybody and signalled them to move out.

As they started to march out of the small grounds, the doors of the ambulances burst open at the back and several soldiers jumped out.

'Oh my God!' shouted Leyla and turned around to run back. Doctor Ibrahim held on to her and pushed her forward.

'What's wrong with her?' shouted a soldier.

'Nothing. Nothing,' said Ibrahim. 'Just a little unwell. She will be all right.'

Into Leyla's ear he added. 'For God's sake Leyla, do you want us all killed? Just walk on. We will get out of this. I promise you.'

No sooner had he finished talking then shooting was heard coming from the hospital buildings. Leyla looked around and saw smoke coming out of its windows. She heard glass shatter as she saw the legless body of one of her patients hurled out of the top floor. She turned her face away with tears in her eyes. She found it hard to walk. Sheer terror at what was happening kept her legs working almost independently of the rest of her.

'Who's the lovely whore?' shouted a voice from behind a tree. A man came out and walked up to the commander who put both hands out. He slapped the outstretched hands jovially.

'Which one?' the commander asked disinterestedly.

'The one with the big tits,' answered the first. He walked up to Leyla who held on to Ibrahim's arm.

'Is it a Palestinian cunt then?' asked the man laughing.

'No,' answered Ibrahim. 'She's Egyptian'.

'Can't she speak?'

'She's frightened.'

'Nothing to be frightened of here sister. We're not after your people. We're only looking for Palestinian shits.'

He walked away laughing.

'I am!!' shouted Leyla.

'For God's sake Leyla!' implored Ibrahim.

The man turned around and looked at her.

'You're what?' he asked.

'She's frightened,' faltered Ibrahim.

'I am a Palestinian!!' growled Leyla.

The man came forward and took her arm. He pulled her out from the others. Ibrahim tried to hold her back. One of the soldiers came forward and hit him across the face with his gun. As he fell the man started to kick him.

'Fucking Palestinian lover!' He stepped back and pulled out his gun. He pointed it at Ibrahim's face.

'Open your fucking mouth!!' he screamed.

Ibrahim looked towards Leyla and nodded. The revolver slipped into his mouth as the gunman laughed.

The commander shouted at him. 'That's enough. Let him go!'

The soldier stopped. He helped Ibrahim up and left him standing there unsteadily. Leyla looked at him and smiled. She mouthed some word at him.

'What did she say?' asked one of the soldiers.

'Jerusalem,' answered the one who was pulling her away. 'What is it with those people and their crappy Jerusalem? You want to go there sister? Come on. I'll take you to Jerusalem. Jerusalem. Jerusalem. Let's go.'

* * *

'Hey brothers. Look what I've got me,' shouts the man as he gets halfway down an alleyway.

Several men and women come out of a small building. They walk around Leyla admiring her beauty. One woman touches her face and strokes it gently.

'She's good. Good,' she starts to coo. 'Shall I get her ready for you?'

'Yes. I'm gonna have me a great night tonight.'

They all laugh as three women lead Leyla away. They take her into a small room. In the corner sits an old man who has been shot through the temple. Behind is a bed and he is half leaning against it.

'Now listen little flower,' says one of the women. 'Listen to the advice of a big sister. You can do this the hard way or the easy way. If you co-operate they might let you go. See what I mean little sister?'

Leyla nods. Her face is stained with tears. Other than that she looks completely cold. Inside her she is in turmoil thinking of a way out of this. What would Tamra do now? What would any woman do? Fight? Leyla knows that to do so would only make things worse. They do not kill you in cases like these. They have their fun other ways. She knows from her hospital experience what rape victims are like. Those who fight are the worst off.

'Undress then dearie. Show us your treasures.'

Leyla starts to undress slowly. She takes her clothes off and lays them neatly beside the dead, old man. She folds her bra and puts one cup into the other and lays it on the old man's lap. With an apologetic look; she removes it and throws it on the bed.

'She's a neat young lady,' says one of the women.

Leyla stands in the middle of the room and looks at the ground. One of the women comes forward and lifts her face gently. Her gentleness surprises Leyla. The woman smiles and pats her cheek. Her other hand goes between Leyla's legs and grasps her hair. She laughs as she gives an almighty pull that sends Leyla screaming to the floor.

The other two laugh. One of them pats her friend on the shoulder and says, 'Don't damage the goods, love.'

The woman bends and touches the pendant around Leyla's neck.

'Forever? Your boyfriend?'

'Yes,' gasps Leyla. 'Yes. One I love a lot.'

'Good. So you've had experience in this business. I knew you were all fucking whores. Well my girl you're going to know many a man before the day is out.'

The three women leave the room and stand outside.

'She's ready boys,' sings one of them.

Suddenly there is an eruption of gunfire and the joyous sounds of men shouting and clapping. A man walks into the room and shuts the door behind him.

'My God! I didn't expect this. You're a real beauty sister. A real treat.'

Someone knocks at the door and shouts, 'Come on, hurry up. We've got rights too.' Several people start laughing outside.

The man unzips his trousers and takes out his erect penis. He looks at Leyla who turns her face away. He goes up to her, wrenches her face towards his penis and shouts, 'Suck it, you lovely whore!'

Leyla shuts her eyes and, taking his penis in her mouth,

starts to retch.

The laughter outside suddenly comes to an end as abruptly as it has started. The place becomes ominously silent. The man looks around him, withdraws from Leyla's mouth and walks to the door. He opens it a little. His face lights up as he hurriedly pushes his penis back into his trousers.

'Hey boss look what I've got. Come on in here and look boss.'

He opens the door fully. Leyla covers her breasts with her arms as she remains kneeling near the bed. At the door stands Pierre. He looks at her for a few seconds. Suddenly he seems to recognise her.

'Out! Out!' he shouts at the man.

'Okay. Okay. The boss wants to go first,' he says as he walks out. The others laugh and fire their guns in the air again.

'Leyla?' asks Pierre after a short silence.

'Yes sir,' she whispers realising whose face it is behind the large and bushy beard.

Pierre looks around the room several times. He looks back at Leyla.

'Lie on the bed,' he orders.

Leyla steps over the old man and lies down. Her face is to the wall. She hears a rustling sound. She knows that Pierre is getting undressed. She tries to think hard of what to do or say next. Outside the others would help him. In here: it is worse.

She takes her pendant off.

'What are you doing?' His voice is above her now.

'Sir. This pendant. Tamra . . .' She does not finish her sentence. He plunges his knife into her heart. She gasps, looks around and grasps both his hands. Her eyes look into his.

'For Marie!' he says as he pushes further.

He unclasps her hands and lets them fall beside her. Her body gives one last shiver before it settles with its hand on the old man's cheek. Pierre removes the pendant from her and looks at it. He puts it in his pocket and leaves the room.

THIRTEEN

Pierre returned home in triumph. His eyes gleamed with the pleasure of vengeance and release. Marie was at peace. He walked into his house and hugged Tamra. She smiled to see him so happy.

'Daddy,' she had not called him 'daddy' for such a long time. 'It's lovely to see you so happy. Have we won the national lottery?'

'Better. Much better my child. Come. Sit by me,' he said as he patted a seat beside him. Tamra sat down feeling heavy at heart after what she had heard on the World Service of the Sabra and Chatila massacres. Mixed with this heaviness was a happiness at seeing her father so pleased with himself for the first time in over five years.

'What is it daddy?'

'I was at Sabra. I was there and we made them pay for all they have done to us. We've really made them pay. The bastards!!'

'Oh God!'

'Yes Tamra. God is on our side in this. We did his bidding.'

'Please no more father. Please. Please tell me you weren't there. Not you daddy.'

'But I was my child. I was and I loved every minute of it. It is only the beginning. There won't be one of the motherfuckers left in our country. Not one shit.'

Tamra looked at her father and saw his wide open eyes glare into space. His bottom lip trembled with excitement and he kept rubbing his hands together. A sliver of spittle played at the corner of his mouth. Tamra saw that this was not her father. This could not be the same man who had saved so many lives at Karantina. Not her father. Nor Marie's husband.

'"Speak, stubborn earth, and tell me where, o where hast thou a symbol of her golden hair" . . . "Your mother loved him. She will rest in peace now. All's well". "Yet she had, indeed, locks bright enough to make me mad". Ah Tamra, your mother is happy now. She saw it all. And I brought you a special keepsake from that fucking whore. I stopped them fucking her. They were lining up to do it to her, but I stopped them. Here. This is for you,' he said as he held out Leyla's pendant to his daughter.

Tamra gasped as she stared at the word 'forever' swinging back and forth. She snatched it from her father.

'Wear it my child. It'll bring you luck. It released your poor mother's spirit. Wear it. 'Her pearl round ears, white neck, and orbed brow'. Ah see! See! Marie loved that fellow. I know him by heart.'

'Oh my God. Father. Father. Why? Why Leyla?' she screeched moving away from him.

'Why? Why? Because "my spirit clings and plays about its fancy, till the stings of human neighbourhood envenom all." Your mother is at rest. No poisoned neighbours for her.'

Tamra reached the door and stood trembling with her hand on the handle.

'You're mad. You're all mad!'

'Mad! No I shouldn't think so my dear. "Unto what awful power shall I call?" No we're not very mad.'

'Father she was the sweetest and kindest of women. I loved her, father.'

'So did I my child. So did I. But her soul is now at rest. Do you remember: "Beauty is truth, truth beauty, that is all ye know on earth; and all ye need to know." Do you remember?'

'Oh God, get me out of this Hell!!'

'Go on holiday my child. Go with Paul. Good man. I like him. As God is my witness. Her soul is at rest.'

'Oh father, you poor, sick, raging animal. I shall never forgive you for this,' she whispered across the room. She hurled the pendant at him and screeched, 'May you all rot in Hell for what you've done to us. All of us.'

She ran out of the apartment and into the road without aim or purpose.

* * *

By the time Tamra had reached Sabra, the Israelis had withdrawn. There was nothing left but the civil defence contingents clearing up. The stench was overpowering. Long gaping holes had bodies lined up in them with lime covering their features. Tamra had no chance of finding Leyla. She asked several people around Leyla's house if they knew anything. They told her that they knew that Leyla's parents had died.

'And her brother?' she asked.

'He got away with the wounded. He was all right.'

'Where did he go?'

'How the fuck should I know, sister?' flared a young man standing in the midst of the group.

Tamra walked away. A woman went after her.

'You must excuse him, sister,' she explained. 'He didn't mean to be rude. He really didn't mean to use that language. Forgive him.'

'That's all right. I understand.'

'He's lost his son. He can't find him anywhere. He was a baby. He's found the mother. She is over there,' she added pointing to the mass grave. 'But his son has disappeared.'

'I hope he finds him . . .'

'Oh no. No. He's dead They burnt bits of him after chopping him up. They also fried other bits. Not much left. Not that you'd recognise anyway. But I'm not telling the poor fellow. Let him have a little hope for a while.'

'Dead? How do you know?'

'I saw 'em do it,' announced the woman half proudly. 'I saw 'em my sister.'

'Do you know Leyla Salman? I'm looking for her.'

'Everybody knows Leyla. She was an angel of mercy. Wouldn't leave the wounded in her charge so the bastards killed her. What I want to know is where were the fucking Arabs?' she suddenly started screeching. 'Where were the fucking Arabs when all this happened? Where?' Then she whispered to Tamra, 'One day we will get our revenge sister. One day. We will my dear sister . . . But you must excuse him for using a dirty word in front of a lady like you. Ladies like you don't belong in a fucking awful place like this. There's so much bad language here!'

Tamra went to Leyla's hospital but found no one who could tell her anything about her friend. The hospital had been partially burnt. Corridors were filled with the victims of the previous night's carnage.

As she left the camp she took one last look as if hoping to find Leyla somewhere. She could not think of the real possibility. She could not sink it into her mind that her dear, dear friend had died. Had been killed. Murdered. By her father.

'This is niggertown Tamra. And niggers are flattered by the attentions of a white woman who would grace their hovel with her presence.'

Tamra left the camp and drove towards the university. Israeli jeeps went by her going in the opposite direction. Some soldiers waved at her. She ignored them as she thought of Leyla.

'I love you as I would a sister born and bred with me. And I know how you feel about me. Our love is strong. Our friendship will always last.'

Tamra drove towards the beach entrance to the university. She remembered it as it was when she and Leyla studied there. Despite her recent research work there, she wanted the AUB to remain hers and Leyla's.

'But we're not above all this, love. We're not. One day this place is going to explode into some awful carnage. When it does; I, as a Palestinian, would be on this side of the divide; while you would be on the other side. It's not inconceivable that your gun would fire the bullet that would kill me or mine.'

Tamra reached the university and parked the car on the beach road. She walked into the campus and tried to think of her old days there.

'Look at this pendant. I shall continue to wear it until my dying day. One day we will laugh at ourselves for crying now.'

'I love you Leyla,' whispered Tamra to herself. 'Will you ever forgive us?'

'I love you too. More than you can ever imagine.'

Tamra had reached Leyla's old building housing her little room. She went upstairs and knocked on her door. Somebody called out, 'Come in' with a broad Palestinian accent. Tamra's heart almost stopped at the sound of Leyla's voice. She opened the door and looked in. One the bed sat a very young girl with a pretty little face. She was busy manicuring her toe-nails.

'Hello,' she said cheerfully.

'Hello,' answered Tamra. 'I'm sorry to disturb you. I've got the wrong room.'

'Never mind, love, I'm used to it. The boys from engineering are always getting the wrong room.'

Tamra smiled and started to close the door.

'Bye,' sang the girl inside.

'Bye,' answered Tamra.

Tamra returned to her car on the beach. She walked across the road from the car and looked into the blue shining water. It was very blue. It reminded her of that last happy morning with Paul.

'You have beautiful eyes. The colour of the sea.'

She wanted him now more than ever before. She felt a strong sense of regret at not having accepted him then on the beach. They were young then. Life was spacious and free. It would not be the same now. Too much had happened. There was so much to do. So much to rebuild. She remembered Mr Shah's cryptic joke.

'To build bridges . . . We've got the bridges. It's the water under them that we can't forget.'

'The sea is beautiful, is it not?' asked the same voice from behind her. She looked around and saw Mr Shah standing there looking out at the water.

'Mr Shah!!'

'Call me Mr President please. I'm not using that other name anymore since my business here is no longer a secret.'

'Yes Mr President,' she replied politely.

She wanted desperately to get to a phone and call Paul.

'I must go sir. I have an important telephone call to make.'

'Beware. Beware. They listen to every word you say. Be careful. Best not to use that infernal machine. If you have to then speak in code.'

'I'll be careful Mr President,' she said as she walked away.

She re-entered the university and went to the girls' hostel. As she walked in she caught a glimpse of Nasser walking behind her and stopping just outside the building.

She dialled Paul's number in the hotel area. When he came on the telephone he sounded breathless and very excited.

'Tamra! Where have you been? I've been looking for you everywhere.' His voice was conciliatory and slightly frightened.

'I've been driving around.'

'But the place is crawling with Israeli soldiers, love.'

'Paul what is it? What has happened?'

'Nothing. Nothing. I was worried about you. I kept looking for you.'

Tamra knew that he was lying. What could be be hiding? Leyla's death? She wanted nothing now: nothing except him.

'Oh Paul darling! I want to be with you. I want to come to you. I love you.'

'I love you too Tamra. I always have. Where are you?'

'At the university.'

'Wait for me there. I'll come for you.'

'No. I'm coming to you darling. You wait. Please.'

'You can't come to me love. The seaside road is closed. You'd have to go the other way. I don't like . . .'

'Please Paul. Please. I will come to you.'

There was a short silence. Tamra could hear him breathing fast.

'I'll be there before you know it.'

'All right. But be careful.'

'Paul?'

'Yes darling?'

'I love you. I want to be with you. I'm sorry I wasted so much time.'

'I'm sorry I did too. I'm sorry about this war. I'm sorry about everything that didn't go right. Tamra, listen. We'll go to Geneva. We'll go to our lakeside cafe. I'll go with you. I'll go where you and I can be together always.'

'That would be lovely. We could have a long holiday.'

'I wasn't talking about a holiday, darling . . .'

'You don't mean?'

'Yes. Yes. I mean we'll leave. I've had enough. I've done enough. I want you now.'

'I want you too, darling."

'I can't wait till you get here. Hurry up. I'll get the necessary papers sorted out for us to leave. Hurry darling. I want you in my arms.'

'We've waited long enough. Another half an hour is not going to kill us.'

'Isn't it?' Paul laughed. 'I don't know about you; but I sure as Hell have been waiting long enough. I'm still dreaming of your glistening body by the sea. Do you remember?'

'I wish I had said "yes". I wish we . . .'

'Don't wish for anything that's gone. Let's look ahead.'

'I won't be long.'

'Be careful.'

'Don't worry. Now you've got me I don't think it will be so easy to get rid of me.' She laughed and hung up.

As Tamra came out of the building she saw the President standing in the same place. She ran up to him and kissed him on both cheeks.

'Oh Mr Shah I'm so happy. So happy.'

'Mon enfant, you've done well in Physics.'

'Mr Shah?'

'Shshshsh! President Nasser if you please. I will accompany you to your limousine.'

He held out his arm. She entwined hers in his and they walked out of the university for Tamra's last time.

FOURTEEN

Beirut sank into a darkness darker than its unseeing eyes. Rain-soaked streets reflected a drab moonlight that seemd to do little to light up the blackness of the early night. Deformed and misshapen buildings were silhouetted against a darkening sky. Complete swishing silence covered the city centre, by now accustomed to its own solitary unquestioning existence.

The only difference between day and night were the shadows. At night shadows were still there but could not be seen. Like colours; they only appeared when reflected by light. At night the only light available in Beirut was imagination. The dead had none of it. And the living were far far away from that sinister black centre.

Now and then something scurried across muddy and watery roads. It did not make enough noise to indicate a human. It sounded more like a large cat. It would have passed for a large cat were it not for its long narrow tail with its distinctive ratness. Well-fed rats survived the worst excesses of the recent siege. Massacres suited their stomachs and the stench filled their nostrils with a longing for more.

Amidst this watery darkness moved a large being. Not a rat. Something bigger. Much bigger. Like primeval man just learnt to walk erect: it shuffled, grunted, and murmured to itself and into the darkness.

It splished sploshed its way down a main thoroughfare covered in overhanging large plants through years of neglect and decay. The rats shot here and there in fear. Some stopped, looked intently at the strange creature, turned and ran.

It was horrible.

A perfect picture of the moon slithered away from its centre to the edge of the little pond. And there, standing in its place, whitened by the feeble light, stood the creature.

It had large deeply set eyes with a thin film of horror across them. Its face – if face it was – was elongated by a busy straggling and dirty beard with gingery patches curling away. It had no nose to speak of. Its mouth, though, was cavernous and noisy as it breathed wetly in and out. Dressed in rags; the creature's feet were caked in mud, sewage, and blood.

Now and then it let out a howl that sounded like a frightened dog. The creature would raise its arms up at the sky, turn its head far back, open its mouth, breathe in deeply and let out a terrifyingly long ear-piercing howl that frightened even the rats out of their death filled habitat.

One hapless rat scurried into the water. Quick as a flash; the creature was upon him. It managed to catch the rat by the back of the head. It picked him up, took him by the tail, and splattered his tiny brain against the wet ground. Once. Twice. A thud with a loud puffing sound as of a tyre loosing air filled the place.

The creature stood holding the dead rat above its head and cackling. It jumped across the watery battle field clutching the late rat.

Oscillating towards a half-standing wall; the creature sat down to enjoy its hunted meal.

The dark, black, eternal void was filled with the wet slopping of blood and chewing of raw meat.

* * *

After Tamra left her father's apartment; Pierre sat in his frontroom staring ahead and drinking. Hours later, overtaken by an overpowering sense of loneliness without Marie; whose soul no longer spoke to him, he walked out of the apartment block and drove towards the seafront. He suddenly felt an urge to find Tamra. To salvage from the little pretence of sanity appearing a new return to the old relationships within his family. He realised that with Marie's soul gone to its eternal resting place; his only living relation was Tamra. He had to find her.

He went to Paul's headquarters to ask him to help. He was out. Pierre left an urgent message telling him that Tamra had gone and that when Paul found her he should get in touch with him immediately.

He drove towards the sea front entrance to the university. He knew that this was one of Tamra's favourite haunts. He would look there and then go into the University itself searching for her.

He drove around without paying any attention to the Israeli soldiers who had just moved into West Beirut. A few times he was stopped and asked for identification. In all cases, the Israelis smiled at him and let him go. He was one of their allies.

As he drove along the seafront he saw yet another roadblock ahead of him. He started to slow down with exasperation. He had little time for such idiocies. His mission of finding Tamra was taking on supreme urgency.

'Look my friend,' he shouted out of his window as he slowed down. 'Look. I've already been stopped at least five times. Please let me through. I've got to get to the airport road quickly.'

A young man without a uniform came forward. He knocked on the passenger side window of the car. Pierre wound the window down. Quickly, the man unlocked the door and jumped in digging his machine-gun into Pierre's ribs.

'Don't worry brother, you won't be stopped again. Just

drive!'

Three men jumped in the back. One of them had a belt of grenades strapped to his chest. He was smoking a massive cigar. The other two sported huge bushy beards. It seemed as if their faces were only covered in hair with small slits for eyes that wandered all over the place suspiciously.

'Now my friend. Just drive back where you came from. You won't be hurt. We just want a little chat.'

Pierre turned the car around and started driving towards the port area and into the city centre. He felt his brain clear itself of its drunkenness as terror crept in. This was a kidnapping and he knew that he would be lucky to get away with his life.

'Where are we going?' he asked, his voice hoarse with fear.

'For a little ride my friend. That's all. Now don't be so frightened. We're not going to hurt you. We just want to have a little chat. Okay?' The three men in the back of the car giggled and one of them clapped his hands merrily like a five year old.

The car turned the corner into the Place des Martyres after which it could go no further. It was late afternoon with dusk just beginning. Pierre stopped and sat behind the wheel waiting for his captors to move.

'Right friend. Step outside,' said the man in front.

'What do you want?' he squeaked unable to speak properly. 'Take the car. I've got nothing else on me. Take the fucking car and go.'

'No my friend. No need for naughty language here. We want to chat, that's all. We are not thieves. We just want to ask you a few questions. Okay?'

'Show me your identity card, little friend!'

Pierre handed his card with trembling hands. The man looked at it and smiled amiably.

'This shit gentlemen,' he started announcing at the top of his voice. 'This shit is a fucking Christian. Gentlemen, I put it to you that he has no use for his balls!' He started laughing loudly, showing a row of clean white teeth.

'Shoes! Shoes!' prompted one of the other men.

'Shoes?' asked the first. 'I thought that it was balls. I've read the play too.'

'No! shoes. Balls come in the next act.' They all laughed except for the one who had sat in the front of the car. He walked up to Pierre and kicked him with all his might. Pierre double up retching violently.

'Right! That takes care of the balls. Now take off your shoes you Christian bastard! Take them off before I blow your brains off.'

Pierre quickly took his shoes off and handed them to one of the men. They went flying as far as the man could throw them.

'And your socks, please,' said the leader with mock politeness.

Pierre peeled his socks off and dropped them on the ground. Clapping his hands again, the drugged man shouted, 'And trousers! And trousers! Everything! Everything!'

Pierre stood staring at his captors.

'No!' he shouted imperiously. 'No!' And he stood holding his head as high as it would go. The men looked at him with surprise. The leader stepped forward again. Pierre flinched awaiting the kick. Nothing happened. There was a long silence as the man stood staring at him. The other men waited aside to see what was going to happen.

'Now listen well my friend. I'm going to give you a chance. I'm going to let you get away. Do you see that building over there? I'm not going to start shooting till you get there. There's a chance that you can make it. If you do, then you're the luckiest motherfucker I've ever met in this delightful little war! Now, what say you?' He stared at Pierre who looked back at him with resignation in his eyes.

Suddenly Pierre turned and started to run. As he did so, he heard several shots fired ánd almost felt the bullets whizzing by his head.

'Stop! Stop now or the next will go right through your head,' shouted the leader. 'The race has not started yet!'

Pierre stopped. He did not dare turn around. He stood still waiting for the inevitable to happen.

'You start when I say 'Go!,' shouted the leader laughing for the first time.

A short silence followed. Pierre heard a rustling sound behind him followed by a whistle going through the air. Something hard hit him in the back. He looked around to see several stones flying towards him. Several hit him in the face and shoulders. He fell.

'Go!' shouted the leader.

Pierre stood up unsteadily and started to run. He could see the designated building getting nearer and nearer as stones kept landing beside him. Just before the building, there was a mound of rubble. He ran as hard as he could and dived behind the stones. As soon as he hit the ground the air was filled with the sound of shooting and the smell of gunfire. The shooting continued for a while. It came nearer and nearer as Pierre started crawling towards another hiding place. The shooting stopped.

'You cheated,' shouted the voice. 'Cheat! Cheat! We're not playing anymore.'

Pierre kept crawling frantically. The stones he crawled over cut him badly. He was aware of sharp pains everywhere. His terror made them seem as if they did not belong to him. He crawled faster. He stood up and started running again. As the shooting increased he dived into the building designated by the leader. He collapsed in the front entrance to catch his breath.

'Cheat!' shouted someone. 'Throw him a few bangers!'

Pierre got up again and ran well into the building. As he reached an exit at the back several explosions took place. He kept running. Jumping over a wall, he emerged in an alleyway overgrown with grass and various plants that had smashed their way through the asphalt and concrete. He knew that he would be safe there. He sat huddled in a corner and waited.

At a short distance, he could hear his followers laughing and clapping. A few minutes later he heard the unmistakable sound of his car engine start. A screeching of tyres was followed by hooting and men screaming and shouting.

Pierre fell back exhausted with running and terror. He closed his eyes as he felt several sharp pains all over his body.

When he opened his eyes, he did not know how long he had been sleeping. It was dark and slightly chilly. The buildings were silhouetted before him. An almost full moon allowed him to see a little bit and he got up stumbling his way around the ruins. He felt desperately thirsty. The pains and distant aches were becoming more acute. He walked towards a pool of water in the middle of the alleyway. He fell onto his stomach and dipped his hands in it. He gently pushed the surface dirt away and started to cup handfuls of water into his mouth. The water tasted refreshing and cool. He drank more and more as he felt the coolness spread inside him. The more he drank the more he realised that the water tasted bitter and a little gritty.

He got up and walked towards the Place des Martyres. He passed a little shop with its front blown open. He entered in search of food. It turned out to be a fabric shop. He gathered as many rolls of cloth as he could get and made a bed. He fell into the heap with a tumbling heaviness. Feeling nauseous, he closed his eyes and tried to sleep away the nausea.

When he woke up again, he could see daylight filtering into the shop through the broken front. He tried to get up, but felt a burning cramp shoot through his stomach. He lay back again. The pain suffused itself through his body and out. He tried to get up again but the pain shot through him and he lay back.

He wondered if the water had poisoned him. He kept asking himself if this was it: death creeping slowly from within him. Trying to get out to visit others in this hapless and unlucky country. Hapless? He asked himself. How much of what happened here had been our fault? How much of it was pure self-destruction?

His mind went back to the days before the war. In his wildest dreams he never imagined when he returned from the U.S., that life was going the way it went. He remembered when he first married Marie. Those were romantic days. Not that he had shown much romance. But it was there. He felt it. On their honeymoon they had spent a blissful week together in a chalet in the Cedars. They went for long walks, made love, and sampled the excellent local cuisine. They had no worries. He thought of the time they made love in the shower. Marie had been reluctant to start with. She had been shy. Not of him. Just shy. Young and frightened of what they were about to do. And he made love to her in the shower. Afterwards, they sat on the deep carpeted floor and kissed for ages. He kissed her all over as he felt a strong and uncontrollable sense of urgency take hold of him. He had turned her over and taken her second virginity as she moaned and urged his body on. There was no shame then. Just love. In these war torn days, even a kiss was shameful. There was no longer any love.

One night they had driven down to Baalbeck to see a British company put on Othello. Marie had enjoyed the evening. And he, like Othello, had enjoyed it for her. And he too loved too well but not wisely. He never had a real partner in her.

Now, lying amidst the ruins of his country and of his life, he realised how futile his insistence on tradition had been. Where were all the traditions now? What was it all about now as he lay dying in the ruins of a shop he would have been too proud to frequent during peaceful days?

He had always imagined his death coming in old age

with his ageing wife and his grown daughter standing beside his bed with him amidst clean white sheets. His head resting and his eyes staring at their beloved faces imparting a last life-important message on the edge of life.

He closed his eyes and tried to sleep. He felt cold. His legs were getting numb.

He dreamt of Baalbeck with Marie. They were sitting in the audience watching Othello. In the background he could hear the distant echoes of Beethoven's Choral Symphony inexorably drawing his soul away from the other. He tried to cry out. He could not. He looked at Marie sitting transfixed to her seat enjoying the play. He put a hand out to touch her but could not reach. His soul rose higher and higher and he could see the whole valley. The massive Roman ruins looked like a small toy town. Marie was no longer there. He flew over the mountains with their snowcapped peaks and swooped down onto Beirut resplendent with lights and bustling with life.

He could not control his soul's flight as it crashed into the heart of the city. People looked up and could not see him. He called out to them to catch him. No one heard. As he crashed, Beirut's lights went out and he was surprised to feel no pain.

He woke up with a start in the darkness of the shop. The moon threw its white light in through the cracks and onto shelves of clothing that resembled a group of mourners standing by his bed. He called out for Marie.

He tried to sit up slowly awaiting the pain in his stomach. Nothing happened. He got up and walked gingerly towards the door. Suddenly his whole body seemed to do a somersault as he retched and bent over vomiting with excruciating pain. He did not seem to be able to stop as he felt his body separate itself from his will and empty itself of its many impurities.

* * *

The heat of pain in Pierre's head subsided after his meal of raw rat. He retched again and held his head in his hands grunting and trying to scream but failing to do so.

He headed back towards the clothing shop. One more night's sleep and he thought that he would be all right.

He walked into the shop and felt his legs getting lighter. Whatever it was that had struck his body was obviously going, he told himself. He explored the shop in the moonlight. He wondered why no one had looted the material in it. Probably no one in his right mind would come into this area with its gunhappy snipers. Even then, he thought that the snipers might have made a few pounds out of this place.

He screamed when he first saw it. Before him stood an ugly creature with deeply set eyes and a long gingery beard grunting and breathing heavily. Pierre stepped back in horror as he recognised his own reflection in the mirror. He stood still staring.

The moonlight made his reflection look even more ghostlike than his yellowing skin made him anyhow. He felt a searing heat go through his brain as he stared at himself.

The reflection smiled at him. It moved its head up and down and made a sad, tutting noise.

'What has become of us?' it asked quietly. 'Look at us my friend. We are like animals. Is this the face that smiled at Marie when making love? Are these the hands that stroked her body? Look at us my friend. Look!'

Pierre raised a large bale of cloth and hurled it at the figure before him shattering it to pieces. In the cracked bits of mirror. Pierre saw a thousand little reflections of his face. Distorted and pained.

He put his hand out and grabbed a sharp piece of mirror.

'Go away!!' he screamed as his brain burnt and his body seemed to wilt beneath his heavy soul.

'Go away!!'

He plunged the piece of mirror into his chest over and over again. As he folded into a sitting position he frantically stabbed his wrist in a series of quick sharp strokes.

He opened his eyes and looked at the shattered mirror before him. The ugly figure had gone. He breathed a sigh of relief as he felt his blood ebbing away warmly and fast. His brain felt less painful. Heat escaped replaced by a stony refreshing coolness.

'What's the use?' he whispered into the air. 'It was all for nothing. Nothing!!'

He slid backwards and shut his eyes.

'Marie!'

As darkness was replaced by strong burning sunlight such as he had never experienced before; he saw Marie stand before him. On her face was her eternal smile. She was years younger. As she was when they first married. Beside her stood little Tamra holding her hand.

The little girl looked up and saw her father. She ran towards him.

'Daddy! Daddy!'

'I'm here,' whispered Pierre as he opened his eyes and saw the darkness of the shop. He quickly closed them again and was relieved to see Tamra still running towards him.

He opened them again briefly emerging into darkness and closed them for the last time with Tamra's singing voice ringing in his ears.

FIFTEEN

Tamra knew that her only way to the hotel area was through the city centre. She was not frightened. She had little time to think of any dangers that might be lurking there. She drove her car until she could go no longer. The streets were deserted and dirty. Grass and weeds sprouted out of the asphalt. A few bouganvillaeas overgrew and spread over the precarious walls. One half destroyed-wall looked as if it was held up by a massive bouganvillaea exploding in red-purple colours. Pockmarked walls stood, every hole with something to say. The silence around Tamra was only disturbed by her footsteps.

In the distance she could see thick mist covering the snow capped mountains. Although it had stopped raining, the atmosphere was heavy with dampness. It was not really dark yet but night was already falling. Tamra thought that the surreal scene before her bore no connection to her happy state of mind. This war had nothing to do with her anymore. It was not her war. She had found her victory in him. He was waiting for her.

She could hardly wait to get there and fall into his arms. Why had she waited for so long? Why did she not accept him long ago when she knew that she loved him? Why not? Because of some stupid promise made to her protective and caring mother years ago? Where did that promise fit in with all the death and destruction around her? A promise made as a compromise. And compromise had no place in Beirut any longer.

Of course she was her own woman. She knew that she herself had made this choice. It had nothing to do with the urgency of war. In years to come she would be able to work this thing out. It did not matter now. All that mattered was getting to him.

'Beware of snipers!' The sign was clumsily written and planted askew in the hard soil.

'You shouldn't be going that way, sister.' The speaker appeared from nowhere. He was short and somewhat squat. He said the word 'sister' in a very suggestive way moving his head forward as if to inspect beyond his listener's outside. He looked at Tamra as a doctor might a patient. His whole demeanour was saying, 'Look, I know what lies beneath your being. Your soul is an open book to me.'

For a short while Tamra felt frightened. Was he on his own? She had heard enough horrific stories about gangs of men and women who lived in destroyed houses and roamed the streets at will. Snipers seemed to leave them alone as if they had their own code of honour. Snipers shall not kill rapists. Rapists shall not rape snipers.

'You shouldn't go that way my dear,' he smiled at her. She pointed towards the general direction of the seaside and said, 'I must get there before nightfall. It's urgent.'

'Are you from the Red Cross?'

'Yes. The Red Cross have sent me. I'm urgently needed. There are several injuries in the hotel area.'

'Ah yes. I was there the last time. The battle of the hotels everyone calls it now. Awful.' He spoke to her in a chatty tone of voice as if they were standing over the garden fence. 'I used to live there many years ago. Before your days I dare say. We still had trams then . . . But you can't go that way. The place is full of mad snipers. Wait till the morning.'

She was about to answer when a massive explosion took place down the road from them. 'Rockets!!' he shouted.

Gunfire suddenly started somewhere near where they stood. Tamra looked around for its source. The man grabbed her hand and shouted to her to follow him. They ran towards a building that stood at the other side of the road. As they entered it a shell landed so near that Tamra thought they were about to be hit. It was as if their movement had been spotted and the snipers were having a cat and mouse game with them. She felt anger rise within her. There was no fear. Just anger at the thought that someone was stopping her from getting to Paul.

The man pulled her into the building and raced down some stairs. They were obviously heading for an underground shelter. It occurred to her to let go of his hand and run out. She could still take her chances outside. Heaven knows what fate awaited her in the underground. The man's grip tightened as if he knew her thoughts.

'Come with me sister. We'll look after you.'

We? Who were we?

A group of rapists?

Suddenly Tamra felt frightened. She pushed the man away and ran up again. He called to her to stop. As she was halfway up the stairs a flash went before her eyes and she felt a piercing pain in her ears. She fell backwards into his arms and could feel herself half carried half dragged down. She fainted with a strong sense of relief.

'Is she all right?' asked the man. Tamra felt dizzy as she lay in a badly lit room with a woman bending over her.

The woman smiled gently and said, 'You're all right love. Do not worry. You've had a terrible shock though. What made you run away like that?' Tamra did not answer. She lay looking at the woman's young face. It appeared tired and somewhat worn. But she still looked attractive.

'What's your name, love?'

'Tamra. And yours?'

'Nadia. This is my husband. And those two little horrors are our boys,' she added affectionately pointing to two boys sitting in a corner of the room.

'I didn't realise anybody still lived here.' Tamra was still unsure of her hosts. She could not understand why anyone would still want to live in this horrible area with the stories that were going around.

'I'll be damned if I'm going to leave my house because of a few gunhappy thugs,' answered the woman laughing. 'You must rest a little. You can't go on now. They're really at it tonight. Must be a special night. New delivery of arms. Must try 'em out!' The woman was unbelievably cheerful as she spoke. There was little fear in her voice.

Tamra's eyes wondered around the room. It was well furnished. If it were not for the shooting that she could hear outside she would have thought herself in some typical bourgeois home in Ras Beirut. Everything was spotlessly clean. The only things that indicated a state of siege were several large bottles of water and a latrine discreetly hidden in one darkened corner. There was a musty smell. The place had not seen fresh air for a long time.

'How do you live?' asked Tamra without really wanting to know. She felt an awful need for sleep. Yet she knew that the panic rising within her was caused by her worry about Paul waiting for her. He would be worried by now. He might decide to go out looking for her. At least he would not come into this area since she did not tell him exactly which way she had decided to come. But then he probably knew that this was the only quick way to him. He knew Beirut better than even she did.

'How do you live?' she repeated.

'Like everyone else in this city,' the woman said smiling again. She seemed to smile mechanically. Years of experience in the art of making others feel better showed through her smile.

Nadia turned around and called the two boys. They came forward and shook hands with Tamra. One was no more than six and the other must have been about ten. The ten year old looked slightly frightened and ill at ease.

Tamra shook hands with them and smiled. She ruffled the little one's hair. He had large, innocent eyes. He smiled back at her.

'Nadia, shall we get something to eat?' asked the man quietly. They moved away from the bed and started getting a few things out of a cupboard hanging on the wall. It looked like the best of kitchen designs. They put a few things on the floor beside the bed. Nadia started a primus up and put a kettle on. There was something comforting about the whole operation.

The little boy produced a little figure and showed it to Tamra.

'Oh how lovely. Who is it?'

'Action man. Daddy got it for me. You could make it talk by pulling the string. Here in his back. But the string broke.'

'That's a pity. But you can do the talking bit, couldn't you?' The little boy nodded. Tamra looked at his elder brother and smiled.

'Have you got something nice to show me?'

'Yes auntie.'

The boy ran across the room and returned with an album. He sat beside Tamra and opened it. It was full of postcards of scenes from Lebanon. Some were old, yellowish ones from early this century. The boy was talking very fast about each one while his little brother stood staring from the top of the bed.

'This is one of the Place des Martyrs before the war. Look, you can see hundreds of cars and people. There's the statue. I've got one of the statue on its own. Look.'

Tamra remembered the statue. She had seen it many times. She had never particularly liked it. Yet she could not help being moved by its majesty. She approved of the representation of the risen woman. It was strange how women all through history were used to represent rebellion against corrupt authority.

Looking at the pictures made her feel a nostalgic sadness for the old Beirut. Even at its most chauvinist it bore the hallmarks of vitality and the illusion of continuity.

'Many of those houses aren't there anymore. Daddy says that one day Beirut will be beautiful. They're going to build it from scratch. There will be big parks everywhere. I'm going to study engineering and help rebuild Beirut. When I grow up.' He smiled confidently and looked to his father for approval.

They all sat around the bed with the food in the middle. Tamra raised herself on her arm and turned on her side leaning over as she made a pretence of eating whatever was offered to her. Nadia encouraged her to eat and to drink some hot tea. Although Tamra did not feel like eating, she did as she was told. She did not feel that she had the resistance to do her own thing and go to sleep.

There was something odd about their little island of peace in the midst of the shooting and carnage outside. This family were a sign of hope for a brighter future. Tamra was relaxed for the first time in a long tiring day. She was like someone just pulled out of a raging sea into a safe and sturdy boat.

Nadia told her about their life since the war started.

'We used to live in an apartment upstairs. When everybody had gone, we moved down here and have been living here ever since. My husband still works for the Ministry of Telecommunications,' she added proudly. 'He is one of the heroes who maintained a telephone service all through the civil war and the bloody invasions. There were times when he was trapped at the telephone exchange and we didn't see him for days.'

She told all this with a cheerful tone. Here was a true story-teller, except hers was a true story. Their life unfolded before Tamra. It was much the same life that she had led for a long time. The only difference was that these were people who suffered the daily brunt of the civil war. Hers was sheltered compared to theirs. These were the people that she imagined existed but never thought could really be there. She did not want to believe that her compatriots were so humiliated. Made so low. Living in underground burrows like frightened animals. But Nadia did not seem frightened as she jovially fed her family.

After they had finished eating everything was cleared up by the whole family. The gunfire outside had become occasional. The atmosphere inside was almost festive. Tamra felt relaxed enough to kiss both boys good night and turn over to go to sleep. The boys slept on clean mattresses in the corner. Tamra slept awhile, waking up with a start. She heard Nadia laugh behind the door as silence returned. Tamra turned over.

'I love you,' the man's voice came through the darkness.

'I love you too,' answered Nadia.

As Tamra started to doze off, she could hear subdued gasps from the corridor. She smiled to herself to think that she and Paul were not the only lovers in this dark, sinister city.

Tomorrow she would be with him.

* * *

'In the name of the Father, the Son, and the Holy Ghost. Amen.' Tamra could just hear the end of the family's prayer as she woke up. It occurred to her that they had never asked her what her religion was. She felt grateful for that.

Nadia spotted her and asked, 'How're you feeling dear?'

'All right.'

Tamra got out of bed and steadied herself a minute. Her ears felt a little strange; otherwise she felt good. Today was the day she would be with Paul.

'Look,' said the husband. 'We'll have breakfast and I'll walk you to the hotel area. Are you sure that you want to go there? It isn't really safe.'

Tamra nodded vigorously.

'I can get you there,' he added cheerfully.

They left the underground shelter after Tamra kissed

the boys goodbye. Nadia hugged her and said, 'Be careful. You are in good hands. If anyone could get you there, he could. He knows Beirut like nobody does.'

Tamra smiled as she saw Nadia exchange proud glances with her husband. She felt happy at the thought that she was never likely to return to this place. Paul was waiting for her. A new life was waiting with him.

'Come and see us again. Anytime you feel like it,' added Nadia.

All was quiet in the sunny city centre outside. Somehow everything was more cheerful this morning. The overgrown wild plants that seemed to be eating away at the buildings yesterday were all bright and colourful today. Tamra spotted the huge bougainvillaea hanging off the collapsing wall. Its little triangular redness spread everywhere.

They walked together without talking. The man was tense as he used every muscle of his body to gauge his route. He obviously knew every alley and every corner. Eventually they reached the Place des Martyrs. The statue in the middle of the square was badly damaged. Tamra remembered how she used to get taxis from the rank beside it. This used to be a happy and busy square. Day and night it was alight with busy people and moving cars. Now it stood empty and silent. At a distance it looked like a giant, badly-kept football field with grass everywhere. Tamra could imagine how one day it would return to its old glory. She wondered how many people would ply their business in it without ever thinking of its silent, deathly days. She wondered if people in Hiroshima ever stopped to think that they were walking, talking, sleeping in the same place and the same ground and under the same sky but in a different time zone. In another zone the devasation was still there. Just as Beirut would be one day.

'Stop exactly where you are!!' shouted a voice. Both stopped and looked around. Out of the shell of a building stepped three men. Not men really but boys looking like men. None of them could have been more than sixteen or seventeen years of age. Two of them carried Kalashnikovs and the third carried a lute which he was strumming happily.

'Who's the whore?' asked one of them.

The man turned pale and answered roughly, 'She's my daughter!'

'Your daughter, eh?' asked the one with the lute. 'Let's have a dance then.'

Tamra heard the crackle of a Kalashnikov and saw the smoke rise out of its barrel. Her escort gurgled and fell forwards almost in slow motion. His body seemed to fold up rather than fall.

Tamra screamed and ran. She heard the boys laugh and shout after her.

'Don't go sister. We're not going to hurt you. Come back. Let's have some fun.'

She heard another crackling sound and felt a sharp, piercing pain down her back. She collapsed and rested her head on a small grassy mound. She could see the whole square stretch out before her as her eyes clouded over. She said something.

'What did she say, Einstein?' asked one of the boys.

'Didn't catch it.'

The other boy with the Kalashnikov laughed and spoke loudly, 'Out looking for fuel, I expect. I wouldn't have minded pumping this one myself boys.' They burst out laughing. He pushed her dress up to her stomach. He tried to unroll her underwear and only succeeded in half doing so with one hand.

'Shit! Why'd you have to shoot her? What a waste of a good screw!! What a waste of woman power . . .' he said prodding his Kalashnikov against her vagina. 'Look at it. It's almost sucking the gun in!! God! She's a fucking beauty . . .'

'First time I heard that word used in its correct sense. Come on man!! I'll find you another living doll,' shouted the musician.

SIXTEEN

Paul did go out looking for Tamra. By the time that the sun had set, he got several of his companions and they all set out looking for her in the city centre. The group broke up into three parties and set out in different directions after agreeing to meet at dawn back in the hotel area. Paul's headquarters had been moved into an underground shelter after his building received several direct hits from the Israeli Air Force.

Paul's team headed for the Place des Martyrs and looked into every shelter without success. They found several stragglers hiding in various places. They encountered no particular difficulty to start with. There were too many of them and they were well armed.

They met a man who told them that he had seen a girl fitting the description that very afternoon.

'She drove to the post office building,' he added.

'Which way did she go?' asked Paul.

'Shit! I don't know. She was walking over there. Slowly. She was looking around like a bloody tourist. I didn't take much notice. She might've gone to the Place des Martyrs. That's the general direction anyway . . .'

Paul thanked the man and gave him some cigarettes. He and his group went back and covered every inch of the ground.

As they approached the Rivoli cinema building gunfire broke out around them. Trained in not panicking; they dived for cover efficiently and returned fire. There was no obvious area to fire at. Like a great deal of Beirut's gunfights; men and women simply shot at random.

There was something exhilarating about the sound of gunfire to most of them. To Paul it felt unreal. Rather like watching a western when one did not feel like it. It was impossible to suspend disbelief. Beirut was becoming more and more like a distant film. The danger was there, death was there, the shooting filled the air; but the audience knew it was a pleasant hoax. Now and then a spectator stood up to pursue normal life and ended it with a bullet through his head or neck. They never collapsed. They always seemed to crumble; as audiences did in cinemas with a bag of pop corn in their lap.

Paul wished he were out of it. After so many years it was enough. They had proved nothing. At one point they thought themselves heroes fighting for a homeland. They were all fighting for a homeland. But somehow the homeland refused to recognise their sacrifice. They died and suffered for nothing. They did not fight for a homeland. They fought, as far as Paul was concerned, for some faceless arms dealer swimming in wealth. They fought for foreign powers: powers like Syria, Israel, the U.S.A., Russia and Heaven knows what. But they were certainly not fighting for the homeland. The homeland had had enough. And so had Paul.

The battle intensified. Rockets were launched. Several Katyushas landed away from Paul's group. In the dark there seemed little point in fighting. But fire they did. This was a ritual that most Beirutis had grown accustomed to. At the same time Tamra was looking through the little boy's postcard album and worrying about Paul.

The group remained pinned down for a long time. Some person was obviously trying out his new infrared Israeli army issue. It was never a sure thing that the person shooting was a Phalangist since several weapons changed hands either through death or simply through business transactions by clever war profiteers.

As dawn approached Paul managed to assure himself that his group of five women and eleven men had survived. He shouted across the square for a parley. Somebody shouted back they they were ready to stop at a price.

'Name your price,' shouted Paul.

'What do you have?' asked the voice.

Paul asked around and found that he could raise some five hundred Lebanese pounds and about thirty dollars. He told the voice what he had.

'We'll have the dollars. You can shove the pounds.'

There was a short silence. A few minutes later a youthful figure appeared from the left. He was a young lad carrying a lute which he strummed as he walked towards Paul. The strumming got louder and louder as he got nearer.

It was difficult to place the tune. It was badly played. The instrument was old and out of tune. It created an atmosphere of madness and strange incongruity. Paul almost expected to be lifted with the lute player up into the air to look down on Beirut. They would fly around and look at those little dots shooting each other. And once they were dots; would it really matter what happened to them? The smaller the dot the less feelings it seemed to carry within it.

'Dollars my friend. And the road is all yours.'

Paul handed him thirty-two dollars. He bowed and motioned them towards the bottom of the square. They started to walk away from him. Some backed away and others walked with their backs to him and his hidden companions. They were not particularly fearful of being double-crossed. Money never broke its promise in Beirut. Otherwise, how could one do business?

'Hey! Seventeen of them! Seventeen men and women! Hey Einstein! How many each at thirty-two dollars the lot?' he asked no one in particular.

'About a dollar ninety each,. Mozart,' shouted a voice from the left.

'Thanks Einstein. One dollar ninety. The market is really depressed these days boys. One dollar ninety. That makes it just over ten dollars each for us my little kiddlings!'

Several of Paul's people turned around.

'There are only three of the bastards. Let's blast them to Hell!'

'No!' shouted Paul. 'Walk away. Now!'

His men and women were surprised by his vehemence. They looked around at him. He tried to smile.

'Look. We're out to look for Tamra. Please help me find her. Then you can have your balls blown off if you want!'

'Sexist!' said one of the women. The others laughed. Some of them waved at the lute player.

'Hey Mozart! Play us a tune,' shouted one of them as they walked off.

And the dots moved away amidst the ruins. On one side several small black dots picking their way through rubble. Behind, left standing alone, another dot. From it came the strains of continued unintelligible strumming.

* * *

Seated in his headquarters, Paul was inwardly panic-stricken. On the outside he remained as calm as possible as he telephoned all over the place in search of Tamra.

His other groups returned and told him that they had found nothing. Telephone calls were made to the Red Cross and the Red Crescent. Nothing. He tried many hospitals. Paul knew that he had to use up every favour owed him to find Tamra. He phoned various old friends and acquaintances on all sides of the war. The Palestinians promised to look into it for him for old time's sake. The Phalangists said that they would send a party out to look for her as soon as they heard the name Shami. Several street thugs and their allies presented their help for a price. Paul said yes to anybody who came. He offered a reward of ten thousand dollars to whoever finds her alive. There will be no money if she were found injured or dead. He added this to stop various street gangs putting a price on her head dead or alive.

By mid afternoon, some news arrived. One of the women searchers came to see Paul.

'We've got a woman who's lost her husband. She had Tamra with her last night.'

'Bring her here!' ordered Paul.

'Can't. She's gone with the others to look for him. We've got her two boys though.'

'Where're they?' Paul went to another room where the two boys sat looking very frightened.

'Would you like a coke, boys?'

The boys nodded. As they happily clutched their bottles of coke, Paul got all the information that he needed.

He ran out of his office into the strong sunlight. He started running as fast as he could. Behind him one of his men tried to join his boss. He could not keep up and was soon left far behind.

As Paul turned the corner into the road leading to the Place des Martyrs, he saw one of his jeeps racing towards him. He waved them down. There were several men hanging on the outside of the jeep. They jumped off just before it stopped rather than face him. He knew what this meant.

'Where is she?' he shouted. 'Where is she?'

'She wasn't there chief. She wasn't. They'd already taken both of them away. The Red Cross had just picked them up . . .' screeched one of his men. Paul looked around in despair. Every face told him the same story. He could not accept it. He did not want to accept it. Not Tamra. Who would want to hurt her? This sort of thing never happened to the people one loved. It happened to others. Not Tamra. Not Tamra!

* * *

Paul was a man demented. He would not accept Tamra's death. He kept thinking that it was his fault. Had he only insisted on her waiting for him instead of forgetting himself in the joy of becoming hers.

He walked from hospital to hospital in search of her body. Whatever happened, he was going to find her and take her where she had always wanted to be: on the beach. He would take her privately. It never occurred to him to think of her dead parents. As far as he was concerned Tamra had always been his. Since her birth over twenty years ago she had been his and not that madman Pierre's. Orphaned: she only had him now. Just the two of them. Nothing else. Not even any feelings of revenge. Just a loss.

He went to the American University Hospital.

'No woman of that description passed here. Sorry.'

'Are you sure?'

'Look, I told you. We haven't seen her. For God's sake go! I've been at it for two days. Look at the corridors outside. For fuck's sake I feel as if I'm working in some horror movie. . . Go. Look for yourself.' The doctor's bottom lip trembled slightly. Paul patted his shoulder and walked out.

As he walked around the hospital he did not stop to look at the dead and dying lying in the corridors. Several people sat on the floors waiting to be treated. There was little distinction between the seriously injured and the others. They all sat silently. Now and then there was someone who moaned or called 'mother'. The others would look towards the source of the moan and then look away in embarrassment. They all had wide glazed eyes. Pitiful taut mouths tried to smile at him as he passed by.

'Is he the doctor?' someone asked desperately as he clutched an unconscious child in his arms.

He went to several private hospitals to no avail. He did not want to admit the fact and go to the city mortuary. To go there meant that he had irrevocably accepted her death.

After exhausting all night searches he headed towards the mortuary. The caretaker there was an acquaintance of his and treated him as a host would a visitor to his home. He smiled at him and welcomed him in with an offer of a cup of coffee. There was a very strong stench in the place. The kind of smell that Paul associated with the city abattoir where he first learnt about the Palestinians. In his heart he no longer had a place for hatred. Hatred of Palestinians or anyone else disappeared and was replaced by his overwhelming obsession with finding Tamra.

'I'm looking for a young woman. She has – had long, blond hair and . . . and . . . blue eyes. Was one brought in here last night or this morning?'

The caretaker thought hard scratching his head. Suddenly his face lit up like a school boy making a new discovery in a Science lab. He smiled broadly.

'You're in luck my friend. I've got just the one you want. She was brought in early yesterday morning. Shot badly she was poor child. About twenty would you say?'

'Yes.'

'This way my friend,' said the cheerful fellow as he led the way into a massive warehouse lined with numerous coffins and draped stretchers.

'She's at the other end. I'm glad you're claiming her. This place gets terribly overcrowded. They don't come in for their folks. Then we have to bury 'em in a mass grave. The relatives come and start swearing at you for not waiting. What am I supposed to do? Would they like my fucking job? Never have anyone to talk to. When the relatives come they're not in the mood for talking. We got to learn from the Irish. Now there's a people for you. You know when theirs die they throw a party and enjoy themselves. Don't take death so fucking seriously.'

Paul was not listening. He smiled absently at the man. Without really thinking about it he did not want to offend the fellow. All he wanted was Tamra.

They crossed the warehouse. At one end of it lay several stretchers with white sheets draped over them. In one case a hand had slipped out of the cover and lay on the ground beside the stretcher. The caretaker bent down and tucked it in tidily while giving Paul an apologetic look.

'There she is. Poor child. There she is. I'll leave you alone for a quiet chat. Then we can arrange transport. Okay my friend.'

'Yes thank you.' Paul knelt beside the stretcher and put his hand forward to remove the sheet. He stopped with his hand still outstretched. He remained immovable for a few seconds. He was trying to blend in with the rest of the warehouse occupants.

He took a deep breath and threw the sheet back.

A beautiful girl lay before him. Her face looked restful and serene. She was not Tamra.

SEVENTEEN

Paul drove back to his room full of unaccountable joy. As long as he had not found her, there may be a chance. He knew that he was deluding himself. There really was no chance of her being alive. She would have been in touch by now. Someone would have called him. What if she were unconscious? What if she had lost her memory? What if she had got out of the country? What if she were in Israeli hands? His 'what ifs' were getting ludicrous but at least they made him feel comfortable.

As he walked down into his underground rooms, he heard someone whisper his name. He looked around and saw a head peep at him from behind a corner up the stairs.

'What do you want?'

'Come this way for God's sake. Come this way. Don't go in whatever you do.'

Paul recognised the voice as President's Nasser's. He really was not in the mood for the poor fellow.

He walked up towards him trying hard not to show his annoyance.

'Good morning Mr President.' He had to make a supreme effort to play the game.

'Good day my boy. Good day. You must not go into your rooms. Mossad agents are lying in wait for you in there. I have been reliably informed by a contact in the C.I.A. that you are on the hit list . . .'

The President cleared his throat self-importantly.

'Thank you Mr President. Thank you. I will be guided by your advice.'

Suddenly the President burst out laughing very loudly. His laughter echoed through the building. He tapped Paul on the shoulder.

'Good fellow. You would be the only one who has ever heeded my advice, my boy. If those Air Force boys listened to me in 1967 we would have won. But no, they knew best and had to ground their forces for breakfast. Yes. Yes. Tragic. Tragic. Well my boy I will leave you now. I am meeting L.B.J. today. L.B.J.. Yes. We have a few ideas to work on. Good day my boy. I shall decorate you one day. One day. And one day son all this will be over. And those who died will not have died in vain. For, to quote a friend, this nation, under God, shall have a new birth of freedom – and government of the people, by the people, for the people, shall not perish from the earth.'

Paul smiled. For a short moment he felt happy for the President. At least he was one man who did not suffer the war now. He lived in another world, another time. The President turned to go. Paul stood looking after him. As he disappeared around the corner it occurred to Paul that this was the one man who would probably be locked up when the war was over.

The President reappeared. He spoke imperiously.

'My boy, one of my agents has sent me word that your agent has been badly hurt. Great pity. Great pity. So young too. Rest assured she will be mentioned in dispatches. Great pity. Never mind my boy. One does not build a nation without blood. Young blood always. We shall visit her as soon as we have finished with L.B.J.. We will of course give her a disability pension. We look after our people. . . .'

Mad as he may have been, there was no one in Beirut who had inside information like the President. He could go anywhere and anytime without being molested. The

President walked off before Paul had time to say anything.

Paul ran after him.

'Is she alive? Is she alive?' he shouted as he shook the President by the shoulders.

The President stood with a look of terror in his eyes. This was soon replaced by a look of supreme disdain and anger.

'Unhand me my boy. Unhand me. Instantly!'

Paul let go of him. He stood back a few paces. His right hand went up in a smart salute. The President immediately responded.

'With the President's permission?'

'Yes my boy. Yes. Go ahead. Ask.'

'Mr President, is our agent still alive? She is a very important agent. She has collected some delicate information that we badly need, Mr President.'

The President smiled and shook his head. He looked at Paul with a face full of sympathy.

'My boy; I'm overlooking your behaviour of a few minutes ago. Battle fatigue. Take a weekend leave. Yes my good man, your agent is still alive. Badly hurt but alive. She has been shot through the back. Shattered the spine I'm told. Awful for someone so young. But she's in good hands. She's with the sisters . . .'

Paul did not wait to hear the rest. He pounced forward, took the President's head in his hands and planted a kiss on his forehead. He saluted smartly and ran towards his car. He jumped in and drove at breakneck speed. As he approached the first corner, he could see the President standing in the middle of the road looking after him and shaking his head.

Paul ran into the hospital and stopped the first nun.

'Where is Tamra? Tamra Shami? She was brought in here yesterday morning. Where is she? Where is she?'

'Mais calmez vous. Voyons. C'est un hopital pas un souk,' reprimanded the nun.

Paul had a momentary thought on how ridiculous it was

to ask for silence in a city like Beirut – and at a time like this! He asked again. This time he was calm.

The nun nodded and took him up two flights of stairs and down a long, clean corridor. After the American University Hospital visit, Paul felt strange walking in a quiet and antiseptic building.

In a small room with only a bed and a sideboard lay Tamra. Her face was very pale and drawn. She was breathing easily and quietly; almost imperceptively. A strong ray of sunlight streamed into the room and onto her bed. Paul knelt by her bed and took her hand. He sobbed quietly as the nun left the room.

'Will she live?' he asked. There was no answer. He looked up and found himself alone with Tamra. He lay his head on her hand again. Her hand moved. He looked up.

'Yes she will,' Tamra whispered. 'Not so easy to get rid of.'

'Tamra, Tamra.'

'Don't let us part again. Let's stay together somewhere quiet and clean. I don't care where . . . Paul . . .'

'Yes! Yes!'